CHILLING ADVENTURES OF

SABRINA

Season of the Witch

A PREQUEL NOVEL BY **SARAH REES BRENNAN**

Scholastic Inc.

For Kelly Link, sinnamon roll and
definite forbidden word, who always knows
how to find strange beauty. Hail Satan.

ISBN 978-1-338-32604-8

10 9 8 7 6 5 4 3 2 1   19 20 21 22 23

Printed in the U.S.A.   23

First printing 2019

Book design by Katie Fitch

Whatever you can do or dream you can do, begin it. Boldness has genius, power, and magic in it. Begin it now. —attributed to Goethe

SOMETHING WICKED

We saw the girl at the edge of the woods in early September. Her red sports car was parked under the trees, and she was wearing a green coat. She looked like a car advertisement that might convince any boy he wanted to buy.

I'm not too bad myself. My aunt Hilda tells me I'm cute as a bug's ear, and she genuinely believes bugs are adorable. I would've mentally congratulated the girl on being airbrushed by Mother Nature and walked on without another glance—if my boyfriend hadn't been giving her so many.

Harvey was walking me home from school. We'd been hurrying before he caught sight of the girl, because the wind was rising. One gust of wind curled around us now like an invisible whip. I watched the first leaves fall from the trees in a sudden bright, beautiful flurry of green. They glistened in the air like a rain of emeralds, and I felt a sudden pang. Summer was so close to ending.

A blanket of thick gray clouds had rolled over the treetops. Greendale was lost to sun and in shadow. Night was coming early.

I nudged Harvey and tried to keep my voice light. "She's hot, but it's freezing out here."

"Hey, she's nothing compared to you," said Harvey. "Nice car, though."

"Sure, you were looking at the car."

"I *was*!" Harvey protested. "'Brina!"

The wind tugged insistently on my jacket as I ran through the new-fallen leaves, as if there were ghosts trying to get my attention. Harvey chased after me, still protesting and laughing. We left the girl in green behind us.

Harvey, Roz, Susie, and I became besties on our very first day of school, in the way kids do: strangers at first bell and soul mates by lunchtime. People said that a boy would stop wanting girls as playmates, and we would lose Harvey as we grew up. We never did.

I've loved Harvey my whole life, and I've had a crush on him almost as long. He was my first kiss, and I've never wanted another.

I remember going on a school expedition through the Greendale woods and finding an abandoned well by a stream. Harvey was so excited by the discovery, he sat on the bank of the stream and sketched a picture of the well at once. I sneaked a look at his dark head bowed over the pages of his sketchbook and wished for him. But I didn't have a coin to throw in the well, and when I tried to throw a pebble in, I missed.

It was winter when Harvey asked me if I wanted to go to the movies. I showed up and was shocked and thrilled to find it was just the two of us. I was so excited, I still have no idea what happened in that movie. All I remember is the brush of our hands as we both reached for the popcorn. Such a simple, silly thing, but the touch felt electric. He reached out and twined my salty fingers with his own, and I thought, *This is how witches burn.*

My most vivid memory of the night is when he walked me home, leaned in, and kissed me at my gate. I closed my eyes, and the kiss was soft, and I was surprised that the whole apple orchard did not transform into blooming red roses.

From then on, Harvey and I held hands in school, he walked me home every day, and we went on dates. But I never brought up the issue of whether we were official-official, boyfriend-girlfriend. Other people call him my boyfriend, but I never have . . . not yet.

I'm afraid to lose what we already have. My family keeps telling me that it can't last.

And I'm afraid he doesn't feel the same way I do.

I know Harvey likes me. I know he would never hurt me. But I want his heart to pound at the sight of me, as if someone is demanding entry to his soul. And I wonder if he settled for something safe and familiar. The girl next door, not the forever girl.

Sometimes I want him to look at me as if I'm magic.

I *am* half magic, after all.

✳✳✳

Harvey left me at my gate with a kiss, as usual. He's come in to say hello occasionally, of course, but I keep my friends and my family apart. I shut the door and moved toward the delicious sugary smell floating through the hall.

"Possum, you're home," Aunt Hilda called out from the kitchen. "I'm making jam! It has all your favorite things from the garden—strawberries, blackberries, squirrel's eyeballs—"

"No!" I exclaimed. "Aunt Hilda! We've spoken about this!"

I stopped in the kitchen doorway and regarded my aunt with horror and betrayal. She stood at our black cast-iron stove, mixing jam the color of blood in a pot the size of a stove. She wore a pink apron that read KISS THE COOK!

She blinked at me. "It's delicious, you'll see."

"I'm sure I'll see," I said. "The question is, will the jam?"

4

Aunt Hilda's mild, sweet face became mildly and sweetly perplexed.

My family don't really understand about mortal palates. When I was young, Aunt Zelda would deliver long, fruitless lectures on how nutritious worms are, and how there are young witches starving in Switzerland.

Aunt Hilda, who is much more easygoing than Aunt Zelda, has always accepted my silly mortal ways with a shrug. She walked over to me and gave my hair an affectionate tug with the hand not holding the red-stained wooden spoon. "My fussy girl. You never want to eat anything that's good for you. Maybe after you come into your full power, things will be different."

Even in my cozy kitchen, the warm air laced with sugar, I felt a chill. "Maybe."

Aunt Hilda beamed at me. "I can hardly believe your sixteenth birthday is almost here. It seems like only the other day when your aunt Zelda and I delivered you. You looked so cute all covered in blood and mucus, and your placenta was deli—"

"Please stop."

"Aw, are you embarrassed?"

"Um, more grossed out."

"It was a beautiful and special moment. Your poor dear mother wanted to have you in a hospital. Can you imagine?"

Aunt Hilda shuddered. "Hospitals are unsanitary. I would never let you near one of those awful places. From the very start, you were my best girl, and I promised myself I'd take care of you. Now look at you. My baby, all grown up and ready to sign away your soul to Satan!"

Aunt Hilda pinched my cheek and turned back to her jam. She was humming as if there was no more charming idea in the world.

This was my family: fond of me, even fonder of embarrassing me, constantly fussing over what I ate and strict about my lessons, always wanting the best for me and expecting so much of me.

Not so different from any other family—except for the dedication to the Dark Lord.

Aunt Hilda's humming died away. "All's very quiet here. Your aunt Zelda is off on a consultation with Father Blackwood, so it's just the three of us for dinner. How is your beau?"

"He's not officially my boyfriend," I said. "Or my beau, I guess, but he's fine."

"That's good," Hilda said dreamily. "He's a sweet boy. I worry about Harvey and that brother of his. In a house with no mother, where a cold man rules, a child pays."

The thought of Harvey was usually a comfort, but not today.

I cleared my throat. "Where's Ambrose?"

"Oh, your cousin is up on the roof," said Aunt Hilda. "You know how Ambrose loves a summer storm."

∗∗∗

I climbed out through the attic to find my cousin.

The sky was black with night and the air wild with leaves. Ambrose stood on the very edge of our sloping roof, dancing and singing to the last wind of summer. There was a cobra wrapped around his waist, its domed head in the place where a belt buckle would be, its golden eyes shining like jewels. He was holding a second cobra like a microphone, the scaly tail wrapped around his wrist. He sang right into its fanged open mouth as he swayed and spun as if the slope of the roof and our gutter was a dance floor. Ambrose danced with the leaves, danced with the winds, danced with the whole night. Leaves whirled down all around him like confetti, and the wind hissed like a thousand more snakes.

I cupped my hands around my mouth and called: "I've heard the term *snake-hipped*, but this is ridiculous!"

My cousin turned, and with his turn the high winds died away from our house. The illusion of the cobras faded away to nothing. Ambrose dropped me a wink.

"I embrace the figurative," he replied. "Literally. Welcome home, Sabrina. How's the wicked outside world?"

When I was little, I always used to ask why Cousin Ambrose couldn't come out and play with me in the woods. Aunt Hilda explained to my uncomprehending six-year-old self that he was trapped in the house because he was being punished.

"Know that his punishment was unfair, Sabrina, and we must love him all the more to make up for that," she'd told me. "It's natural when you're full of youthful exuberance to play little tricks like teasing girls, crashing carriages, drowning sailors, burning cities, ending civilizations, and so forth and so on. Boys will be boys."

It was years before I found out what he'd actually done.

Aunt Hilda has always been indulgent with Ambrose. She's not his mom, he's a very distant cousin, but Aunt Hilda moved to England and raised him when he was young and needed someone. The two of them lived together there for so long that almost a century later, Aunt Hilda still has an English accent. I can picture her coming to care for a tiny Ambrose, magical and filled with maternal care, descending from above like a satanic Mary Poppins.

The spell confining Ambrose to our house has been in place for decades longer than I've been alive. He's always been here for me, haunting the house like a friendly ghost. When I was little, he was the ideal playmate, making my dolls move by themselves and my toys whiz about the room. Now that I'm older, he's like my big and ever-so-slightly bad brother, willing to gossip about boys with me all day long. Or girls, if I ever wanted. It doesn't matter to Ambrose.

I shrugged and walked carefully down the slope of the roof to stand beside him. "The world's pretty much as always."

"Really? From all I hear, seems like the world is changing. Climate change, warlock rights' activists . . . sounds horrible." Ambrose's voice was wistful. "I wish I could see it for myself."

"Cheer up. Our town's pretty much as always. Nothing changes in Greendale."

Ambrose hummed noncommittally. "What's worrying you?"

"Nothing."

"You can't lie to me, Sabrina, I know you far too well. Also," Ambrose said blandly, "I put a spell on you so that if you lie to me, your nose will turn purple."

"You're joking!"

Ambrose grinned. "Am I? Guess we'll see. But for now, tell me your troubles. Unleash every bee in your bonnet. Cousin Ambrose is all ears."

I hesitated. From our rooftop, I could see almost our whole small town, surrounded by trees. The woods stretch on so far, dark and deep. I shivered, and Ambrose put an arm around me.

"Is it your dark baptism? Is it your mortal friends? Wait, no. I bet it's Harvey."

There was an edge to my voice. "What makes you think it's Harvey?"

Ambrose's arm tightened around my shoulders. "Wild guess. I'm wild, and I'm always guessing. And I know how much you like him. Mind you, I'm not saying I understand the attraction. Personally, I prefer my golden boys slightly tarnished."

I poked him in the side. Ambrose laughed.

"So, what's with your boy? Is he in an artistic sorrowful phase? Sweet Satan in a ball gown, I hope he hasn't started calling you his muse."

I thought it over before I answered. There was a worn air about Harvey sometimes, as if he cared too much and had to bear too much.

"He's sad sometimes. His dad and his brother both work in the mines, and his dad keeps pushing him to take some shifts down there too. His dad talks a lot about the family business and the family legacy, but Harvey doesn't want to be trapped down there in the dark."

"Good news, Harvey, mining is a dying industry!" said Ambrose. His voice more thoughtful, he added: "Though things don't stay dead in our town."

"We saw—I feel so dumb saying this, but we saw a really beautiful girl at the edge of the woods. I wondered if Harvey thought she was better-looking than me."

"Impossible," Ambrose said. "Ridiculous. Wait, did you get a picture of this gorgeous specimen? Show me, and I'll tell you the truth, trust me. Well…you can't trust me. But show me anyway."

I pushed my cousin away. "Thanks very much. You're so helpful."

We both sat down on the slope of the roof. Ambrose stretched out his legs. I hugged my knees.

"You think he might be faithless?" asked Ambrose. "I'll cast a spell on him so it feels like his wandering eyes are melting."

"No! Ambrose, you wouldn't!"

I twisted around and glared at him. In Ambrose's dark eyes there was a darker glint for a moment, but the shadow passed.

"Of course not, I'm joking. I'd just do a hilarious and ultimately harmless spell, because I'm a sweetheart. Don't I look like a sweetheart?"

I raised an eyebrow. Ambrose grinned. I made a throat-cutting gesture with my thumb, and Ambrose pressed a hand to his heart as if deeply wounded.

"I guess…I just wish I could be sure of him," I said. "I always wanted to find a great love, like Mom and Dad did. But to have a great love, the other person has to love you back."

My mother was a mortal, and my father was one of the most powerful warlocks in Greendale. I can't imagine how much he must have loved her, to marry her and have me.

"There's a spell for that, you know. Do you have some of Harvey's hair?"

"No, I do not have his hair! And no, *Ambrose*, I do not want to cast a *love spell* on *my man* and *one of my best friends since childhood*, like a *total creep*, thanks for asking."

I spoke in my most severe and Aunt Zelda-ish tones. Ambrose waved a hand in an airy gesture. Leaves fluttered toward him, as if they were butterflies that might alight in his palm.

"I didn't mean a love spell. I'm not a big fan of them myself. They make everything too easy, and I like a challenge. You and I are so cute, Sabrina, anyone suggesting a love spell would be insulting us. But there is a spell that might open his eyes to how wonderful you are. Teenage boys can be so blind. Trust me, I know. I was one."

I could do it. I can do simple spells. My aunts and Ambrose are always ready to help me. Since I was little, they taught me everything they could about the world of magic: I learned Latin and incantations when I was tiny, performed rites to win good luck and find lost things, grew up with the knowledge I must beware of demons and beseech the aid of friendly spirits. I learned the properties of plants in the woods, and which to add to potions and concoctions. But no matter how much I study, they tell me it's nothing to the lessons I'll learn after my dark baptism, when I start going to the Academy of Unseen Arts.

"It's tempting," I admitted.

"Temptations often are."

If I did the spell Ambrose suggested, I could be sure of him. I liked the idea of Harvey gazing at me, wide-eyed, forgetting everything else in the world. I didn't have much time, but I could be sure of him in the time we had left. I banished the private vision with an effort.

"I don't know," I said at last. "Casting a spell on Harvey, for nothing but my own benefit—it doesn't seem right."

"As you wish. You're such a good girl," Ambrose said. "Sometimes I wonder how you're ever going to make a wicked witch."

"Yeah," I whispered to the wind, too softly for even Ambrose to hear. "Me too."

Ambrose stood, dusting dead leaves and traces of glittering snakeskin off his black jeans. "Well. The hour grows late, and I must attend to the late Mrs. Portman, who awaits me in the embalming room."

Our family runs a funeral home. Even witches need to make a living.

Ambrose stooped and tapped my jaw lightly. When I lifted my chin, he gave me a bright smile. "Cheer up, Sabrina. And let me know if you change your mind about the spell."

I nodded, and stayed up on the roof with the storm and my thoughts. The word *late* keeps ringing in my ears. *The hour grows late. The late Mrs. Portman. Late* might be the most terrifying word I know.

Late summer. Only a few more weeks, and then it will be too late.

My whole life, I've known that when I turned sixteen I would go through my dark baptism, write my name in the book, and enter the Academy of Unseen Arts as a full-fledged witch. When I was a kid, I thought that day would never come. I was so impatient to fulfill the destiny my parents always wanted for me, to make my aunts proud, to be a true witch.

My birthday is Halloween, and summer is already coming to an end. I didn't consider, back then, that embracing my destiny as a witch would mean turning my back on my mortal life. Now it's all I can think of: losing my friends, losing Harvey, even losing math class at Baxter High. Every day, I feel like the world I know is slipping a little further out of my grip.

Yet I still love magic. I love the feel of power building in my veins and the idea of having more. I love the click when a spell goes perfectly right as much as I hate the thought of disappointing my family.

It's an impossible choice, and soon I have to make it. I never thought of that when I was a child daydreaming about magic, or when Harvey leaned in and kissed me by my gate.

I guess a part of me still believed that day would never come.

I spent so long thinking the future was forever away. I'm not ready for it to be now.

WHAT HAPPENS IN THE DARK

We are the weird woods; we are the trees who have turned silver beneath a thousand moons; we are the whisper that runs through the dead leaves. We are the trees witches were hanged from. The hanging trees bear witness, and the soil that drank witches' blood can come alive. There are nights the woods bear witness to love, and nights we bear witness to death.

The girl in green that the young half witch saw was waiting for a boy. He came to her at last, through the storm. Many pairs embrace amid our trees, but they did not. Lovers' meetings often end in lovers' quarrels.

"I'm telling you to leave this one-horse town and come with me," she urged. "I'm going to LA. I'll be a star."

The boy smiled a small, rueful smile; his eyes on the

ground. "Isn't that what everybody says when they head for LA? That they're going to be a star. Just once, I'd like to hear someone say they were going to LA to be a waiter."

"At least I'll be something," she snapped. "What are you going to be, if you stay here? Are you going to be a loser your whole life?"

The boy lifted his eyes and stared at her for a long moment. "Guess I will," he said at last.

He turned and walked away, hands in his pockets. She called out after him, her voice raised in imperious, furious command. He didn't answer.

She was too angry to get back in the car. She plunged into the woods and the wind. Her bright green coat billowed behind her as she went; her hood fell from her shining hair, and the wind turned our branches into long fingers that reached to snag her clothes and claws that raked over skin. She strayed from the path and got lost in our woods. It's so easy to get lost in our woods.

She stumbled into a little clearing, where a bright stream ran.

We could have warned her. But we didn't.

The stream shone like a silver chain laid down upon the earth. The howling gale did not ruffle the surface of the waters.

The girl advanced, frowning in puzzlement, and then in the silver, mirrorlike waters she saw her own reflection. She did not see the scratches on her face, or her wild hair. In the mirror of

16

the waters, she had the glamour that only a stranger can possess. She saw someone who was all shining surface, someone who could make you believe the beautiful lie of perfection was true. Someone to be seen once and never forgotten.

She forgot the wind, and the woods, and the world. She saw only herself. She heard only the siren song.

This is the glory you have been waiting for. You were born for this. All you must do is reach out and take it. You were always meant to be special, beautiful, unique; only you deserve to be given this gift, only you, only you—

When the hands reached for her from the waters, the girl stretched out her own hands eagerly for an embrace.

The river swallowed her, green coat and all, with one gulp. The brief struggle barely disturbed those calm, silver waters. Then the girl was gone.

In the living world, the last words spoken about her were *She's nothing compared to you.* It's not an epitaph anyone would want, but that hardly matters.

Now that lost girl is nothing at all: nothing but an echo of a sigh, dying among summer leaves. Leaving behind an echo is tradition. Our woods are full of echoes.

People spend their whole lives waiting for something to begin, and instead they come to an ending.

Well, you can't complain about endings. Everybody gets one.

THE LONELY PLACE

love going to school. It's not that I love Baxter High, the red-brick prison where our football team and their cheerleaders, the Baxter High Ravens, maintain the established pecking order (raven pun intended). It's that I love my friends, and I always have fun with them.

Well, usually.

We have a special table in the cafeteria. The first one of us in the cafeteria always snags it, and people expect to find us there, the inseparable quartet: Susie in her shapeless hoodies, either avoiding the eyes of the football jerks who hassle her or glaring defiance at them. Roz, with her vague stare and strong opinions. And me and Harvey, who always sit beside each other. Normally the four of us chat all the way through lunch.

None of us talk about our families that much. I think Susie's uncle might have problems. Harvey's dad *is* a problem. And Roz's dad is Reverend Walker. It's tricky, having a best friend whose dad is a minister when you have two aunts who might drop a casual "Hail Satan" at any moment.

Usually we talk about books and movies, TV shows and art. Harvey has as many opinions about golden age superheroes as I do about classic horror.

Today, Harvey ate nothing and said less.

"What's with him?" hissed Susie as Harvey carried back his untouched tray. "He doesn't seem interested in anything. Not even Sabrina!"

I tried to smile, and failed. Roz elbowed Susie viciously in the side.

"It's nothing," I said. "We all have off days. I'm sure he'll be a changed man tomorrow."

When Harvey came glumly back to the table, I put an arm around his neck and gave his hair a fond tug.

"Ow!" Harvey exclaimed. "Sabrina, you pulled some of my *hair* out!"

"Wow," I said. "I did not. I was just playing with your hair, in an affectionate and normal manner."

"Sabrina, do you have some of his hair in your hand?" Roz demanded.

I hid the hair. "Sometimes my affections are too strong."

Harvey, Roz, and Susie were all staring at me now. Sometimes I wonder how they would look at me, how strange they would find me, if they knew the truth.

***

No matter what was going on with him, Harvey walked me home as usual. Unfortunately, that meant his eye was caught by the sight of girls in the woods. Again.

"Hey, 'Brina," said Harvey, nodding to the group beyond the trees. "Do you know them?"

There were three girls today. They all wore dresses with lace-frilled collars and cuffs and in dark materials, but with short skirts, like sexy Quakers. There was a boy with them, in dark clothes with dark hair, but I couldn't see his face.

"I don't think so," I said, but I was lying. I recognized the girls, even from a distance. They were a group of three witches who already attended the Academy of Unseen Arts. We've had a few run-ins. Prudence, Dorcas, and Agatha are beautiful, powerful, and not very impressed with the idea of a half mortal attending their precious school. They take every opportunity to make clear that I'm inferior.

Now they were making me feel inferior without even seeing me. Without even trying.

I didn't think I knew the boy. He was probably a mortal they were messing with. Prudence, Dorcas, and Agatha's business was loyally serving Father Blackwood and Satan, and their pleasure was tormenting mortal men.

"Yeah," said Harvey. "I haven't seen them around either. They must be from out of town."

"Are you going to be checking out other girls every day now?" I teased. "Couldn't you have picked a more attractive hobby, like chess or collecting moths? I think collecting moths is very sexy."

"I wasn't checking them out," Harvey claimed. "I'd never do that. It's just that sometimes I do look at people from out of town, and I wonder what their lives are like. I think about how it would be, to leave Greendale myself, and have a totally different life. Do you ever think about that, Sabrina? Having your life utterly transformed?"

"Maybe sometimes," I said softly.

Harvey's gaze was fixed on a far-off vista that nobody but he could see. In some ways, he was a magic maker as much as I was. My artist, my seer of visions who wants to commit his dreams to paper and show the world. He wasn't looking at the witches in the woods, and he wasn't looking at me.

When Harvey dreamed of far-off places, I wondered if he thought of me. Was I in his rearview mirror as he made his grand escape, part of the town and the life he was leaving behind?

As I watched the witches in the woods, the dark-haired boy turned, and a green leaf beside his head caught fire under his gaze. The leaf became a glowing ember and then curled up into darkness. The ash drifted away on the breeze.

Well, well, well. Maybe the boy wasn't a mortal they were messing with, after all. Warlocks were rarer than witches, but there was Ambrose and Father Blackwood and my father, of course. Now I'd seen a fourth. No doubt I'd meet plenty of them when I began attending the Academy of Unseen Arts.

I couldn't let Harvey see witches doing magic in the woods. I caught hold of his hand and pulled him along.

"Come on," I told him. "I've gotta get home. It's urgent."

When I reached home, I ran straight up the stairs and into my cousin's bedroom without knocking.

Ambrose lifted his eyes from a worn copy of Oscar Wilde's *Salome* and lifted his eyebrows along with them. "Sabrina, I might not have been decent. Not saying I'm decent now, in a moral sense, but at least I'm wearing pants."

He was wearing silk pajama pants and a red velvet robe, so it wasn't as if he was ready for an outing. If Ambrose ever had outings.

"Your pants don't concern me, Ambrose! This is important."

"Many people find the topic of my pants to be important and absorbing," Ambrose claimed. He rolled off his bed, tying the gold-tasseled sash on his robe tighter and slipping a dried piece of deadly nightshade between the pages of his book.

I was still panting from my race home and up the stairs.

I couldn't seem to catch my breath, but I said the words anyway.

"Let's do the spell."

Ambrose lit up. "Fantastic! Are you up for a trip to the woods? We're going to need a few special ingredients, since this is a very special spell. Cousin, did you get a sample of Harvey's hair?"

I nodded.

Ambrose smiled. "Good. So we have Harvey's hair, the candle, the rope, the lavender, the rosemary, and the coltsfoot, but we need myosotis. I hear it grows in the woods."

The woods are deadly, dark, and deep. There were once witch trials in Greendale, as there were in Salem, though the Greendale horror was buried and lost to history. Witches died in the Greendale woods, and the hanging trees wait there.

I had never strayed off the woodland paths at night to collect spell ingredients before, but maybe it was time I did. I should become one acquainted with the night.

"The woods..." I said. "Sure."

I didn't have much time before my life changed, and when it did, I had to be ready.

Prudence, Dorcas, and Agatha were always wandering through those woods. I *belonged* in those woods. In a few short weeks, I would be every bit as much a witch as they were.

✳✳✳

I had to venture into the woods by myself, since it wasn't possible for Ambrose to go with me. Luckily, I had an idea for where I could find what I needed.

Harvey had given me the drawing he'd made of the old well we found on our class trip through the woods. I'd taken the drawing home to cherish it. When I ran from Ambrose's bedroom to mine and searched for the picture, I found it neatly folded in the drawer of my desk. When I unfolded the drawing and smoothed it out, I saw what I thought I'd remembered, rendered in Harvey's talented hand, turning the marks of a pencil into living flowers. I saw the tiny petals of myosotis nestled in the long grass, growing by the banks of the little stream.

That felt like a sign.

It felt like less of a sign once I was out in the woods. The wind was not as high as the night before, but the echo of a summer storm was enough to make my coat and clothes billow. I had to fight to move forward, and every tree became an enemy. The boughs rocked so violently in the wind I feared they might break, and whenever they rocked, their shadows leaped.

Above me, I could see only swaying darkness. For all I knew animals could be crouched in those branches, ready to spring, or bodies might hang from the boughs. There were no signposts in the depths of the Greendale woods. There was only finding your way between one shadow and the next.

I was able to find my way.

The abandoned well I had found with Harvey did not look as appealing as it had by daylight. It didn't make me think of wishes granted or love discovered any longer. The well seemed only a circle of stone, its dark eye staring up at the luminous eye of the moon.

Perhaps I had only thought the well was beautiful the first time I saw it because I was with Harvey. I remembered a quote from a story about magic in the woods: *Love looks not with the eyes but with the mind, and therefore is winged Cupid painted blind.*

It was full dark in the woods, leaves veiling the stars. I was almost blind, but as I walked into the clearing where the well stood and the stream ran, subtle illumination turned the grass to threads of silver and the water to a ribbon of silk. The moon must have found a chink in the branches, and now it was lending me light. My aunts say the moon looks down on witches with love.

Even the wind seemed calmer in this clearing. Encouraged, I crossed the shining grass to the riverbank where I'd seen the tiny, pale blue flowers growing in Harvey's drawing. The moon gave me just enough light to make out the flowers growing on the far bank. Harvey's drawing showed flowers on both sides of the river, but it seemed I'd run out of luck.

I crouched down on the bank and tried to reach over the

stream, but I couldn't reach far enough. I stood on the edge of the stream and considered jumping for it.

The stream seemed far wider than it had a moment ago, when I hadn't been thinking of crossing it. I hesitated on the edge, wondering if I should try a leap, or walk down until I found a narrower place in the stream and cross there.

I hesitated for too long. Maybe the ground of the riverbank was muddier than I thought, or maybe the earth crumbled away beneath my feet. Whatever happened, there was one moment of lurching dismay when my outstretched hands flailed and failed to find handholds in the air. I toppled head-first into the stream with a scream that nobody heard.

Silvery water and shadows rushed into my open eyes. Water flooded my open mouth, cold and bitter. I would never have imagined the water would have this wintry chill in summer, bleak as a river that ran beneath a stone mountain and never saw light.

I tried to swim and felt my limbs already numb, my arms and legs leaden weights. I struggled desperately upward, but I was sinking fast. I would never have imagined the stream was so deep.

Then, as I fought for the surface, I felt icy fingers twining with mine.

WHAT HAPPENS IN THE DARK

Every night after Sabrina goes to sleep, it happens.

There is a tree outside her window with a branch that is bare even in summer, stripped of bark, with long, thin twigs that almost seem like fingers. That frail bough sways in the night wind, and the twigs scrape against the diamond-paned glass of Sabrina's window.

Sometimes Sabrina's golden head stirs on her soft pillow. Sometimes her small hands close into fists as if she wants to hold on to something, and she murmurs in her sleep like a child drowsily asking for a kiss good-night.

The birds and the bats, the mice and the foxes, all the beasts that fly or creep near Sabrina's bedroom by night, find themselves straying off course, heading toward her window as if on a mission. Then they check themselves, shaking off the sudden, wild compulsion.

Sometimes Sabrina wakes in the night with a start, pressing her hand against her breast as if she has been suddenly frightened. Her skin has cold dew on it, as if she was abandoned on the grass in the chill of early morning. To comfort herself, she will take up the picture of her father and mother in their wedding clothes that she keeps beside her bed. She will caress their love-bright faces with a fingertip. Sometimes she kisses the picture.

At times like these, the scratching of the branch against the windowpane grows so frantic it is almost a whine. It is almost like a scream.

Danger, my darling.

Sometimes the young half witch comes down to the breakfast table, crowded with her magical, merciless family, and her eyes are heavy. She says that she did not sleep well, but she cannot tell why.

A CHARM OF POWERFUL TROUBLE

The hand closed tight around mine, cold as a drowned man's, tenacious as the weeds on a riverbed. For a terrified moment, I thought that deathlike grip would drag me down.

It pulled me up instead. As soon as I broke the surface of the water, I reached out to grasp the long grass on the riverbank. With the aid of that chill helping hand, I pulled myself out of the stream.

I crawled out of the stream and onto the bank, and found someone watching me.

She was in the shape of a girl, with long hair that flowed in the air around her as if it was water, but her skin was rippling silver. The girl seemed made of mercury, and when she turned to me I saw the blurry image of my own eyes reflected on her cheek and widening in shock.

This spirit was a living mirror, and she had pulled me from the water.

"Thank you," I gasped.

"Not at all. I couldn't let you drown, not when I've been wanting to meet you for so long. You're Sabrina, aren't you?" she asked in a sibilant voice. "The fledgling half mortal, half witch. All the woods whisper about you. And I saw you, with a gathering of young mortals. You walked through this place and discovered the well."

"Oh," I said, light dawning as I realized what she must be. "You're from the well?"

I was shaking with the chill of night air and my soaked clothes, but I curled up on the bank and studied her with the same curiosity that shone in her bright oval of a face. I'd never seen a wishing-well spirit before. Aunt Hilda told me they were shy but friendly spirits who lingered invisibly about wells, hoping to meet a worthy human whose wishes they could grant. My aunt must be right that they were benign spirits, because this one had saved me without my even having to ask.

The spirit of the wishing well smiled, and there were little ripples in her silvery cheeks, like the ripples when small fish swim too close to the surface. I thought they might be dimples. I smiled hesitantly back at her.

"That's right, Sabrina. Do you want a wish?"

"No, that's okay. You've done enough, and I'm just looking for myosotis anyway."

The wishing-well spirit pointed a gleaming fingertip, and I saw the plant growing in the dark grass near my foot, its petals shimmering blue. A trick of shadow must have hidden them before.

"I owe you," I said, and gathered the tiny blue flowers, careful not to crush them.

The spirit's eyes flashed, bright as sunlight on a stream, as she saw the flowers in my hand.

"I believe I know the spell," she remarked. "You wish to open a man's eyes to love?"

"Um. Yes," I said, embarrassed.

It seemed suddenly like the magic equivalent of when Simon Chen got a crush on Roz and spent all his time loudly mentioning that his uncle had a yacht.

The wishing-well spirit regarded me with tranquil, friendly eyes. The wishing-well spirit, I felt, did not judge.

"I'm a little surprised," she confessed. "I would have thought a witch like you wouldn't bother with small spells. I imagined you might be coming here to do a different spell entirely."

A witch like me. The spirit said the words admiringly, when most witches didn't think I counted as a witch at all.

"Do you know many witches?" I asked.

"No," said the spirit of the wishing well. "There are three witch girls who often ramble through my woods, but I never show myself to them. They don't mean well, and I don't wish them well. They're not like you. As soon as I saw you, I wanted to talk to you. I could tell you were special."

I had never thought before about the term *wishing well*, and how that did not only mean a well in which you could toss a coin and a wish. It could mean truly wishing well: wishing only the best for me, as a friend might.

She didn't see something special in Prudence, Dorcas, or Agatha, who thought they were so far above me they might as well have flown their brooms to the moon. She saw something special in *me*. I couldn't help but be flattered.

"What was the spell you thought I'd come here to do?" I asked curiously.

"Oh," said the spirit. "It's a spell you can only do with the waters of the wishing well, to unlock your true potential. Only certain witches can do it. The ones with the potential to be great. When you walked into the clearing tonight, the moon shone behind you like a crown of bone, and the night streamed behind you like a cloak of shadows. I could see you were born to be a witch of legend."

"Wow." I coughed, trying to hide how pleased I was. "I don't hear that every day."

"You should," murmured the spirit. "But I'm glad you found what you were looking for. If you're sure that you did."

A chill needle sliced through the warm clouds wrapping my mind. The hour was very late, I realized. Ambrose was waiting for me. I was scared that he'd worry. I scrambled to my feet, even though I wanted to stay and talk to the spirit a little longer. Maybe hear some more about the spell.

"I did." I lingered another instant. "Thanks again. I wish I could repay you."

The spirit of the wishing well nodded as she sat upon the bank, silver hair twisting about her like moonlit leaves in a wind I could not see. There was something forlorn about her shimmering, slender form. She seemed as sad to watch me go as I was to leave.

"If you want to repay me, come and see me again. It has been so long since mortals visited my well and made wishes for me to live upon. I am so lonely, and there are so many things I would like to say to you."

✶✶✶

I stopped in my room to change clothes and then carried the river flowers to my cousin's door. I'd already decided not to tell him about the tumble into the stream, or the spirit of the wishing well. Ambrose would be upset if he knew I'd gotten in trouble because of where he sent me when he was helpless to go with me or protect me.

Ambrose always tried to play things off and keep the mood light, but every now and then he couldn't help letting a sign of his frustrated fury slip through the façade. Trapping him in this house was as wrong as confining a tiger in a birdcage, and sometimes a predator's eye gleamed through the bars.

Today he seemed glad to have something to do. He let me into his room with a whispered inquiry as to whether the two-headed monster had seen me come in with the goods. I said that was no way to talk about our aunts, and we grinned at each other, a pair of conspirators who knew we were probably going to get into trouble. That was half the fun.

Ambrose took the flowers and laid them out on the table where he'd prepared the rest of the materials for the spell: Harvey's hair, the coltsfoot, a length of old rope, and a special candle. Ambrose snapped his fingers, and a flame leaped from the wick, not yellow and blue but black on black, as if a shadow of a flame was burning.

"They say if someone pure of heart lights this candle, the dead will rise," Ambrose told me, his voice warm and eager. "Sorry, candle, not today."

Necromancy was Ambrose's pet subject. I watched him lean over the table, his dark eyes mirrors of the black flame, alight with magic and mischief.

"Have you ever been in love, Ambrose?" I asked. "Who was the lucky guy or girl?"

"Oh..." said Ambrose, "that's a difficult question."

"Is it a difficult question where the answer is yes or where the answer is no?"

Ambrose shrugged and gave me a fox-like grin.

"It's tricky for witches to love. Perhaps we have harder hearts than mortals. Hard and cold as the highest stone wall, people say. Witches are well-known to be cold and fickle. Maybe it's because we live for centuries, and mortals die so soon. Our hearts must be resilient, because they need to beat longer."

He spoke lightly, but the words settled as heavily on my heart as stones. In the times of the witch trials, mortals used to "press" us witches for confessions. The pressing meant they would pile tablets of stone on a witch's chest until the witch confessed her own sins and the names of other witches in her coven. One of the heroes of Salem, a warlock named Giles Corey, refused to give up his fellow witches. He died, his last words calling out for his mortal torturers to add more weight.

Right now, what I was doing and the thought of what was to come felt like stone tablets on my own chest, making it difficult to breathe. Was Ambrose saying that when I went through my dark baptism, I wouldn't care so much for Harvey and my friends? Was he saying that he and my aunts didn't care as much as I'd always thought—that they couldn't care about me as much as I'd always believed they did?

I didn't want to be crushed under any weight. But I didn't want to be hard-hearted either.

Ambrose was merrily twining flowers through the length of rope. "I don't want to talk about the past. I'd like to be in love in the future! I'd like love to come to me as a great and wonderful disaster. Failing that, I suppose it would be exciting to be captured at sea."

I blinked. "I've never thought of love and piracy as similar things."

I stared at my cousin and wondered how different what we felt was, and what we wanted. If I had a soft mortal heart in a witch's breast, would the dark baptism crush or freeze it?

No. I knew witches could love. I had proof. My father had loved my mother so much that he married her, against all tradition and all law. Their love had been epic, world-changing, rule-breaking. I had always wanted a love just like theirs.

And ever since I was a little girl, in all my daydreams of storybook love, Harvey was my prince.

"I always thought I'd love to be a sexy pirate. Oh well, let's get your love life in order before we address the tragic issue of mine. Knot this rope nine times as we say the words." Ambrose winked as he handed me the rope. "Knot of nine, his heart is mine."

I took the rope in my hands, feeling its rough surface scrape across my tender palms. I thought of the first time Harvey had held my hand, in that dark movie theater, and how our skin pressed together had felt electric.

Strangely the icy touch of the spirit's hand, pulling me from a watery grave, came back to me, more like a shiver than a memory. It felt foreboding. The word *last* occurred to me again. *Last chance to turn back*, I thought.

I tied the first knot in the rope with one swift, decisive movement.

"*Lavender's blue, rosemary's green; she will be loved as soon as seen,*" I murmured.

"*Omnia vincit amor, et nos cedamus amori,*" Ambrose added, the Latin tripping so fast off his tongue I barely understood it, though I'd learned Latin at Aunt Zelda's knee.

"*Omnia vincit amor . . .*" I repeated, stumbling on the words. I tied several more knots, trying to keep up in one way at least.

"*Quos amor verus tenuit, tene—*"

The black flame of the candle leaped, looming suddenly and terrifyingly large. Ambrose smiled in the same way, with leaping darkness. Like a wicked witch.

"Wait," I said. "What was that?" I couldn't hear the last words he'd said. Something about *tenebris,* or shadows, I thought.

My hands were still moving, on automatic. I tied the last knot of rope twined with rosemary, lavender, and the flowers from the river that had cost me so dearly. The rope felt warm suddenly in my hands, as if it were a living thing.

Ambrose's smile was smug. "That was the spell being sealed."

It was done now. I put the nine-knotted rope down on the table and watched the black flame die away. I felt a dull ache and realized I'd bitten down on my own lip too hard. The taste of blood was in my mouth, metal and fear and magic.

"Maybe we shouldn't have done it."

"Magic is what keeps us safe from mortals," Ambrose argued. "Why risk your heart, or anything else? You believe in Prince Charming and happy endings and fairy-tale love, Sabrina, but what happens to witches in fairy tales?"

I looked away from my cousin's dark eyes and darker smile, away from the rope. The flowers I had gathered from the riverbank were bright against the knots, like tiny blue stars, and I thought of the other name for myosotis: *forget-me-not*. I'd always thought of that as a sweet name, romantic even, but for the first time I thought about it as a command. *Forget me not,* even if you want to.

Suddenly it was as hard to breathe, here in my own warm home, as it had been in the stream when the cold waters closed over my head.

It was done, I told myself again. It was too late to wonder what I had done.

"Don't worry so much, Sabrina mine."

Ambrose's voice was coaxing, sweet as poisoned honey, a voice I had trusted and followed all my life. It was much too late for second thoughts.

"You need to get used to breaking the rules, that's all," he assured me. "It's well past the witching hour, and you should go to bed. Good night, fairy-tale princess. May flights of dark angels wing thee to thy rest. You're half human. You should get half a happy ending, at least. I hope your prince will be charming tomorrow."

WHAT HAPPENS IN THE DARK

Rosalind Walker has the strangest dreams.

In the waking world, she's totally normal. The preacher's kid, studious and well-behaved unless she has to fight for justice—and Jesus fought for justice too, so Roz feels that's okay. Her grandma is a little eccentric, but whose grandma isn't? Roz spends all her free time with her family, or with her friends since forever, Sabrina, Susie, and Harvey. Her dad does have doubts about her friends, though.

Funnily enough, Reverend Walker has no problem with Harvey, the only boy in their group. Even though Harvey's brother is the town heartthrob, Roz secretly, guiltily thinks Harvey is just as handsome. Not that it matters. Harvey has always been so into Sabrina there's no way out, thus he's no threat to Roz's doubtful virtue, and Harvey's brother, Tommy, never takes off the cross around his neck. Reverend Walker says the Kinkles are good boys.

Sabrina and Susie are a different matter. Reverend Walker only frowns a slightly puzzled frown over Susie and doesn't comment, but he has a lot to say about Sabrina. Nobody has ever seen the Spellmans in any church.

Roz's dad can get pretty intense, but she can't discard what he says entirely.

Sabrina is Roz's BFF. Best friends forever, the most sacred agreement there is in a teenage girl's life, and most BFFs know absolutely everything there is to know about each other. They constantly sleep over at each other's houses.

Sometimes Roz is scared to sleep at Sabrina's place. She used to think her fear was because of the house being a mortuary, and it is a little freaky to think of bodies laid out, cold and still, beneath the floor Roz walks on whenever she sets foot inside. Roz was once standing in the hall, waiting for Sabrina to come downstairs so they could go, and she had a sharp flash, as if she'd really seen it, of a dead woman lying somewhere beneath her. A dead woman staring up at Roz with open eyes, wide and white and blind.

Where do people go when they die? her father asked Roz once when she was a kid, and she said: *They go to Sabrina's house.*

She still remembers the stern, disappointed expression on his face as he told her that when they died, people went to heaven or hell.

44

They went to heaven if they were good, and believed, and to hell if they sinned, and did not believe.

What goes to Sabrina's house are only the empty shells, after the souls are gone. Roz believes that. She's almost certain she believes.

She still gets a little freaked out even going near the Spellman house, even talking to Sabrina's creepy aunts, and her creepy cousin. Her dad says they are sinners, and Roz senses that, at the very least, they have secrets.

Maybe secrets and sins are the same thing.

Then there are her dreams. Roz keeps those secret. She's a sinner too.

In her dreams there are ghosts in the woods, hanging shadows that swing into Roz's path and stop her from taking another step. In her dreams she sees the Kinkle family with guns, hunting through the woods. She's terrified of Harvey's father, no matter how much Reverend Walker approves of the Kinkles. In her dreams she sees Ambrose Spellman in the mortuary, with blood on his face, laughing. And her best friend, Sabrina, Roz sees her in the woods wearing a white dress that turns black.

And worse than that, worse than anything… Sometimes in Roz's dreams the pictures she sees blur, like destroyed paintings, as if the wet paint of the world is running. She sees herself in a mirror, and her eyes turn to darkness, and darkness drips down her face in long, black trails. The whole world is reduced to messy streaks of color against an overwhelming, all-enveloping dark, and she weeps and her tears are shadows, and nothing makes sense any longer.

Roz loves her friend, and she fears for her, though there seems no reason for fear in the waking world. She's frightened for herself too, and she hasn't told her friends. Not about the dreams. Not about her eyes failing.

She gets headaches, and the words of her father's sermons seem to pound in her head: his voice thundering judgment, so different from his usual low and loving tones. Sometimes Roz thinks those words will split her skull. Sometimes she thinks she will weep blood.

Do you believe in what you cannot see? If she couldn't see at all, what would she believe in? *Blessed are those who have not seen, and yet believe.* What about what she *can* see? Is she supposed to believe in every vision?

She sees things differently, in her dreams. She wonders what other people see in their dreams. Everybody worries that the people around them see things differently, but perhaps Roz worries more than most.

Roz has her dreams, and she has her doubts. On the days after her worst dreams, on the days when the strangest things happen, the doubts get stronger.

She doesn't know whether her dreams are warning her about danger to Sabrina, or if Sabrina is the danger.

DEVILS INTERFERE WITH STARS

went downstairs that morning to find Aunt Zelda staring disapprovingly over her newspaper as Ambrose leaned in the doorway and flirted with the woman delivering our mail.

"You know the saying," I heard him murmur. "How does it go again? Something about good things and packages."

The girl was a redhead, so her blush was extremely apparent, violent crimson under her peaked cap and freckles. We go through a lot of mailmen and mailwomen. I don't know if Ambrose scares them off, or if Zelda requests for them to be changed.

Aunt Zelda came and sat with me at the kitchen table. Usually Aunt Hilda is at the stove, making me breakfast, but not today. I looked out the window and saw the fresh soil heaped on the grave outside. I swallowed and poured myself some cereal.

Ambrose swaggered in a few moments later, passing Aunt Zelda an envelope from the school. It was probably about the next parent-teacher meeting. Aunt Zelda ignored the envelope with total disdain, as she does everything about my mortal life. She was having a cigarette for breakfast, which was standard.

"Really, Ambrose?" Aunt Zelda asked. "A mortal? A mortal who brings the mail?"

Ambrose shrugged and snagged the cereal box from my hand. "It's not like anyone's actually getting attached. I don't meet that many people. What am I meant to do, hit on mourners attending funerals? That would be shocking and inappropriate."

"It would be a shocking and inappropriate thing that you've done many times," Aunt Zelda observed.

Ambrose pointed a spoon at her, grinning. "Yes I have. And I'll be doing it again, Auntie Z." He shrugged and started eating his cereal. "I'm just looking for a connection."

"To what, the criminal underworld?" Aunt Zelda raised her eyebrows. "Why do you need to find connections? Stay calm and worship Satan in an orderly fashion. That's all I ask of any of you. And sit like a gentleman, for the Dark Lord's sake, Ambrose."

She waved her cigarette, held in its gleaming old-fashioned cigarette holder that resembled a tiny pitchfork, in a commanding fashion. Ambrose kept grinning and kept one leg hooked on the back of another chair.

Aunt Zelda consumed the cigarette in a few sharp, short breaths.

"It seems as if you've been wearing pajamas for seventy-five years. Can't you dress properly?"

"Why?" said Ambrose. "It's not as if I'll be leaving the house. Robes and pajama pants are standard hermit attire, and I'm committed to my hermit aesthetic."

I flipped the ends of the little velvet scarf he was wearing around his neck, when he wasn't even wearing a shirt. "So why jazz up the dressing gown with this?"

Ambrose's smile gleamed around his spoon. "Obviously I want to be a fancy hermit, Sabrina."

Aunt Zelda snorted. She herself was sitting ramrod straight, wearing a pinstripe blouse with a dramatically high collar and a double-breasted suit jacket. Ambrose commented once, out of Aunt Zelda's hearing, that Aunt Zelda dressed like an evil secretary pinup. He said he meant that in a good way.

There was a rap on the door knocker, and I smiled. Since the mail had already come, there was only one person it could be.

Aunt Zelda made a small scoffing noise, put her cigarette holder down on the table with a click, and rose.

"I simply cannot deal with mortals before noon."

"Maybe Auntie Hilda will open the door," Ambrose said, his voice deliberately needling. "Or wait, where is Auntie Hilda?"

"She made a smart remark too early in the morning, so I killed her," Aunt Zelda flung over her shoulder as she departed upstairs.

Ambrose leaned back in his chair. "She's in a lovely mood, I must say. How are you doing, cousin? Aren't you excited to see what our spell wrought?"

I kept my eyes fixed on the window, and the fresh grave. Aunt Zelda kills Aunt Hilda every now and then. It's not like it sounds. It's not so bad. She buries Aunt Hilda, and then Aunt Hilda comes back good as new. It's no big deal. Magic can fix anything.

Still...

"I hate it when she does that," I whispered.

Ambrose flicked a hand over my hair. All his gestures are like that, fleeting and casual, his fingers roving like a butter-fly, landing lightly and then moving on.

"I know, cousin," he murmured.

He doesn't like it either, but he jabs Aunt Zelda about it and then lets it go, as if it doesn't matter much.

Witches and their cold, fickle hearts.

It doesn't matter, I told myself, and straightened my own sweater. I'd come home and see Aunt Hilda at the stove, just as always. And right now, I'd see what magic could do for me.

I hopped up. "I should go see Harvey."

"And I'll be entertaining some charming corpses downstairs," Ambrose declared. "By the Dark Lord's drawers, I'm lonely!"

People at school say it must be weird, living with a mortuary downstairs. They have no idea that it's the least weird thing about our family.

I opened the door and saw Harvey standing on my porch. His eyes weren't wandering today. He gazed at me with rapt attention, as if everything from the buttons on my sweater to the buckles of my shoes was fascinating.

"Sabrina. You are golden and lovely as the morning!"

"Um, thank you," I said, and Harvey beamed as if even the sound of my voice was thrilling.

His greeting had been slightly unusual, but I basked in the warmth of his smile and relaxed. Harvey sometimes seemed wistful, or distant, but this morning he was lit up with delight pure and bright as sunshine. It suited him. This was what magic should do: smooth out all the tiny imperfections of the world, and make it right.

"Nice to see you cheerful," I added. "I've been a little worried that something was wrong."

I gave him a kiss and felt him sigh into my mouth.

Harvey said: "Everything's perfect."

✱✱✱

Harvey walked me to every class that day and carried my books to and from my locker. I tried to get a history textbook away from him at one point, and it turned into a bit of a wrestling match. He gazed down at me adoringly. I grabbed on to the book and yanked.

"Harvey," I said under my breath.

He smiled at me brightly. "Sabrina."

"Let *go*."

"Let me do this for you," he told me, his wide, sweet eyes wider and sweeter than usual. "I want to do everything for you."

"I appreciate that," I panted. "But ... let ... go!"

He did let go eventually, though then I sailed halfway across the passageway clutching the textbook. Only a bit of sneaky magic saved me from crashing into the lockers lining the walls.

At lunchtime, Roz, Susie, Harvey, and I sat down at our usual table, and Harvey bestowed his new shining-sun smile on the whole group. The others seemed startled, but pleased.

"Having a better day today, Harv?" Susie asked.

"It's a beautiful, miraculous day," Harvey said earnestly. "Sabrina's in it, isn't she?"

Susie's eyebrows took off as if launched by rockets. "I guess she is!"

We turned the conversation to subjects other than my glorious presence. Harvey was still smiling very brightly, but that was nice. I relaxed enough so that when he went to put his tray away, I said without thinking:

"Hey, could you grab me another cranberry juice on your way?"

Harvey turned to me with a look of horror. I glanced around wildly for the threat.

"You've been sitting here thirsty all this time! You should have said something sooner. I can't bear to think of you suffering."

"I was fine," I said into the silence.

"You are so good," said Harvey. "You sit like Patience on a monument, smiling at Grief."

"Oh my God?" Roz muttered down into her mac and cheese. It seemed less a prayer and more as if she was asking God if he was getting a load of this.

I turned to Harvey and took his hands in mine. Harvey stared down at our linked fingers with soft wonder.

"Seriously, I only got thirsty this minute. It is not a big deal."

He nodded, and lifted one of my hands to his face and pressed his forehead against it, eyes closed as if he was a knight pledging a solemn vow to a queen.

"I would love to get you juice. I would pull the moon from the sky so you could use it as a silver plate to eat your dinner off."

We all stared at him. Harvey beamed and leaped up to get my juice. I hardly dared look at the girls, and when I did Susie's mouth was hanging open. Roz was still staring at her plate.

"I know he's being a little goofy," I said in a very low voice.

"He's always a little goofy about you," said Susie. "This is something else."

I searched hopelessly for an explanation and offered at last: "I think he's having a weird week."

"Clearly!" said Susie.

"When is a week in Greendale not a weird week?" asked Roz. "Harvey is creeping me out."

There was a bitter edge to her voice that made me and Susie exchange uneasy glances.

"I'm not sure I'd go that far," Susie said slowly.

Roz bit her lip.

"Sorry," she said in a stifled voice. "I had bad dreams last night, and I have a headache."

Roz has more and more headaches these days. I mix up

soothing teas for her, but it was time to start talking to Aunt Hilda about making a full witch's potion for her. I could fix this.

"Rest over the weekend, and let me bring in a tonic for you Monday. It'll make you right as rain."

The strained tautness about Roz's mouth did not ease. "I appreciate it, Sabrina, but I'm fine. And hey, Harvey being a goofball is better than him being all mopey like he was yesterday, right?"

She smiled then, and Susie nodded energetically. We all smiled. It *was* better. Magic made everything better.

When Harvey walked me home, he kissed me three times at the gate. "I don't want to be parted from you," he said, his hands in my hair.

"I feel the same way," I told him, and pushed him back a little. "But I have homework to do. You know I don't approve of leaving homework until Sunday! If you do it on Friday, the weekend's free."

"I do know that about you, yeah." Harvey grinned fondly. "I'm still doing mine last thing on Sunday like the Lord intended. See you tomorrow?"

I looked at him blankly.

"The fun fair," Harvey prompted.

In the excitement of spellcasting and my worries about this last summer, I'd almost forgotten that Harvey and I had plans to go to the county fair. People called the day of the fair the Last Day of Summer.

"Oh, right! Yeah, I'll see you tomorrow."

"I'm looking forward to it."

Harvey kissed me again and left me, and I watched him walk away through the woods.

The fresh earth heaped on the grave in our front yard was undisturbed. Aunt Hilda takes longer and longer to rise from the dead these days. Aunt Zelda says it's pure laziness.

I went to the kitchen and got myself a snack. Then I came back outside, perched on a nearby gravestone commemorating a long-ago Spellman familiar, and waited.

It didn't take long before a clenched fist broke the earth, and then a head and shoulders, surfacing from the ground like a swimmer from the water. With a soft grunt and a wriggle, Aunt Hilda rose from the grave.

I wiggled my fingers at her in an awkward greeting. My aunt smiled and gave me a wave back, her face a mask of mud. She tried to brush the earth from her filthy pink dress, but that was a lost cause.

"Why did Aunt Zelda do it?" I asked.

What I meant was, *Why does Aunt Zelda do it?* As if Aunt Hilda might produce a really good reason to temporarily murder your sister.

Aunt Hilda just shrugged. "No harm done, love."

She spoke as if it didn't matter. Maybe it didn't. This was the sort of thing I should get used to, after my dark baptism. Witches dealt in death and the dark arts.

My aunt wiped the mud off her face, gave me a bright smile, and put her arm carefully around me, squeezing me tight without getting mud on me. Aunt Hilda doesn't have a cold, fickle heart, I know that much, but Aunt Zelda often says Aunt Hilda isn't much of a witch at all.

"Let's go inside, shall we? What do you fancy for dinner?"

Her voice was completely cheerful, and her steps sure. I swung myself off the gravestone and followed her up the steps to our house. Aunt Hilda was absolutely right, and she was absolutely fine. Magic fixes everything.

∗∗∗

Aunt Hilda went to bed early. She always says dying tires her out. Aunt Zelda said she was being a baby, but she made her a soothing brew and brought it upstairs. I heard her lecturing Aunt Hilda to drink it. I think that might be Aunt Zelda's way of apologizing.

I sat alone at the kitchen table for a little while, then climbed up the stairs to the attic to find Ambrose.

There was a huge ancient-looking map floating in midair in his room, on paper so old it was yellow and drawn in ink so old it was brown. In gold lettering on the top of the map was written the words *MAPPA MUNDI*. Map of the world.

Pebbles twinkling with mica were flying over the map like tiny stars, pinpointing destinations. In front of the map stood Ambrose, dressed in his red velvet dressing gown and gesturing expansively for the pebbles to move, as though he was a conductor and the pebbles his orchestra.

"Hey, Ambrose."

He flicked a smile over his shoulder at me, then returned to contemplating his map. There were places with the high slopes of mountains sketched out, marked *Here Be Dragons*. There were seas marked *Here Be Serpents*.

I strolled into his room, keeping my voice casual. "What's this all about?"

"I miss espressos in Italy, I miss tea in China, and I miss orgies! Have I mentioned I miss orgies?"

"You have mentioned that occasionally."

"That's because I really miss them," said Ambrose.

I made a humming sound. Witches are dedicated to decrying the false modesty of the false god, and surrendering to all sensual pleasures. I know all that. I just don't know much about it.

I stared at the map.

"If you could be anywhere in the world," I asked, "where would you want to go?"

Ambrose flung his arms out wide. The pebbles scattered

wildly across the room, a contained explosion of brightness, a tiny, trapped Milky Way in an attic room.

"Oh, anywhere but here."

Here, with our family. Here, with me. I've lived my whole life in this house, since my parents died. Since before I can remember. Greendale's always been home. I love it, and I'm scared of losing it: of losing all the things home means to me.

But to Ambrose, my home is a prison.

Ambrose's gaze slid from the map to me, eyeing me side-long. "How is that spell with Harvey working out?"

"Oh, fine, fine," I said hastily. "Yeah, great. Really good."

"Fantastic," murmured Ambrose.

His voice was absentminded. Clearly, he didn't care much. He made another gesture and the sparkling pebbles re-formed, tracing a new path as Ambrose plotted the escape he would make out into the wide world if he could.

"What was the last line of the spell you used?" I asked Ambrose abruptly. "I heard the rest of it, but I didn't catch the last line. What did you say? What did it mean?"

"Oho." Ambrose's mouth curved. "Not able to translate every word of Latin you hear? Off your game, Sabrina? What's next for our usually flawless little spellcaster? If you aren't able to tell the difference between mistletoe and deadly night-shade, Auntie Z. will be *berry* disappointed in you!"

Ambrose always teases me, but tonight his voice struck me as mocking. My eyes narrowed.

"Seriously, Ambrose, I want to know."

"Seriously, Sabrina," said Ambrose, mimicking my voice, deep and stern. Then he broke into a mischievous grin. "I'm never serious. I don't think I'm going to tell you."

"You're not funny, Ambrose."

"*Au contraire*, cousin. I'll have you know I was celebrated for my wit in the French court. The Sun King thought I was hilarious!"

"I don't believe you!"

I turned and left, closing the door with a sharp click. I stomped my way back to my bedroom and sat down on the bed with a creak of my wrought-iron bedposts, sinking into the piled-up quilts.

Not like anybody's actually getting attached, Ambrose said this morning. Ambrose, with his cold, fickle witch's heart. Ambrose can't even imagine truly caring about mortals. Naturally, he doesn't think magically playing around with human love is a big deal.

I'm half mortal, so what does he really think about me?

I shoved that thought aside. One of my school reports said *Sabrina has a very tidy mind*, and I thought that was true. Compartmentalizing keeps everything neat: my friends in one box, my family in another. I love them all, and I don't want my situation to get messy. I like to keep things organized.

These days, I keep worrying that the dark baptism will dump all the things I care about out of the boxes where I've carefully placed them. Everything will be mixed up and muddled and ruined.

I'm attached to Harvey, to all my friends. No matter what happens, I'm going to keep being attached. I have no plans to cut ties.

I sighed and picked up the framed photograph of my parents on my bedside table. It made me feel better to look at them. My father, tall, dark, and handsome. My mother, fragile, blond, and lovely. Like the hero and heroine of a story. A powerful warlock and a humble mortal, but he loved her enough to marry her and have me. I know they loved me too.

Sometimes I dream of how it would be, to live in a different house with no dead people in the basement, to have my father and mother waiting for me when I got home. My mother attending parent-teacher meetings and sympathizing about mortal problems, my father powerful and respected and able to answer every question I had about witchcraft: to have a real family. I love my aunts and Ambrose, but I'd still have them too. If my parents had lived, we'd be a proper family, and I

would never have doubted they loved me. We'd be so happy.
I'm certain of it.

No matter what Ambrose says about witches and their
cold, fickle hearts, I know better. Maybe it's true for Ambrose,
but it won't be true for me.

I'm not like my cousin. I'm like my father. My parents
would have understood.

WHAT HAPPENS IN THE DARK

Death is the darkest place.

Zelda Spellman kills her sister, Hilda, sometimes, and puts her in the Cain Pit in the Spellman graveyard so she will return to life. Hilda tries not to get too cross about it. Zelda would never do it if she couldn't bring Hilda back.

Sometimes coming back is harder than others.

The earth lies heavy on Hilda's breast. The worms slide down her face like tears.

What wakes Hilda up is, she thinks, the same shock of fear that wakes a million mortal mothers. A worry that jolts women from soft pillows and fast sleep, sweat on their faces on a cold night.

Where are my children? Are my children safe?

Hilda's not a mother. She's never had the chance to become a mother. Witches are meant to be slaves to the pleasures of the flesh, and Hilda always supposed she would get around to that. But orgies honestly seem alarming—wouldn't everyone be looking around and judging you for not being as lascivious and flexible as the other witches?—and no man has asked her for her time one-on-one. She's thought about it, of course, especially when she reads a really good book, like *When the Shepherdess Met the Marquess,* or *All Scot, No Waiting,* or *The Wicked Celtic Billionaire's Most Forbidden Secret Baby.* But Hilda doesn't know if she'll ever have the nerve to ask a man to experience carnal joys with her. She doesn't know if she could ever even gather up the courage to kiss a man.

Still, there are children who come first in Hilda's heart, and who have nobody else to care for them. She never expected that for herself. Zelda is the one who obsesses fiercely over babies, who decided (she's always deciding things for Hilda) that they would become midwives. Every baby they delivered, Zelda would touch with possessive love.

Hilda's the Spellman who was always a bit of a disappointment. Sabrina's father, Edward, was magnificent. Her brother always seemed so big, his shadow swallowing Hilda whole. And Zelda is the example Hilda can't manage to follow, unyielding in all things, especially in her commitment to the Dark Lord.

Hilda has no problem with Satan, or magic, or the thrill of woods or fresh blood. But sometimes she envies the mundanes, many of whom take faith easily, who go to their church and worship their false god. Some of them don't have faith at all. It seems terribly comfortable, not to have to believe and serve so intensely. She's never said it, but somehow the coven looks at her and just *knows*. Edward knew, and Zelda knows, and Father Blackwood, the current head of the Church of Night... he definitely knows.

Since she wasn't going to make her family proud like the others, Hilda was expected to make herself useful. So she (usually) does what Zelda says, and she (usually) tries to be a good member of the coven, and she cares for the Spellman orphans.

When witch-hunters and tragedy struck Ambrose's family, Hilda was there in England to pick up the pieces and look after the child.

She remembers little Ambrose years and years ago, toddling across cobblestones that Hilda's long dress and petticoats swept over. He would dash fearlessly out into any danger, and she fretted constantly that he might be run over by a rattling carriage or drown in a duck pond. But she could never leave him behind, even when she went out on an errand, could never resist his huge, beguiling eyes or the little hands lifted entreatingly up to her. *Auntie Hilda, pick me up, take me with you, Auntie Hilda, carry me!* Ambrose liked to be perched in her arms, held up high to see everything that he possibly could. *Your eyes are too big for your stomach*, mortals say about little ones who want to eat more than they can manage. Ambrose was always greedy for the whole world.

She remembers Sabrina, saved by a miracle from the devastating crash that killed her parents. Sweet baby Sabrina, her tiny face framed by ruffles and ribbons, rocked in midair by magic as Hilda sang a witch's lullaby.

> "Rock-a-bye baby, on the treetops
> When the wind blows, the cradle will rock
> When the bough breaks, the cradle will fall
> Baby flies over a village and curses them all."

Hilda's heard the mortal version. She thinks it's barbaric. There will be no fall for her darlings.

Hilda has always been the least important of the Spellmans, but to a child with nobody else to look after them, you can be the most important person in the universe.

But she couldn't seem to do anything right. Even caring for a child, Hilda got terribly wrong.

You spoiled Ambrose, and look what happened, Zelda told her when they decided to take Sabrina in. *You ruined that boy. You will not make the same mistake with Sabrina. I will take the lead with*

Sabrina, and I will make her a shining darkness for the Spellman
family. Try not to get in my way and wreck everything again.

Ambrose doesn't seem ruined to Hilda. He's still her sweet boy, who teases her and makes her laugh and takes her part against Zelda. But there are no two ways about it: He committed a crime against their kind and was sentenced, bound to their house for "conduct unbecoming in a warlock."

Zelda says he's disgraced their family. Hilda wouldn't mind that, but her Ambrose, who wanted to eat up the whole world, is trapped in their house. He tries to laugh about it, but she sees his mouth quiver even as he laughs. She knows he must feel as if the walls are closing in. Hilda sometimes feels that way, and at least she can go to town and have a browse through the bookstore. The bookstore owner is rather a dashing man.

She worried that Ambrose would be jealous of Sabrina when Sabrina came to live with them. But Ambrose always treated the baby with careless affection, as though she were a pet. When Sabrina was small enough to carry about in Hilda's arms, Ambrose would kiss her little gold head as he flittered by in his restless hummingbird way. Sometimes Sabrina would catch at his clothes or his ringed hands with her tiny fists, relentless even then, and Ambrose would seem amused as he allowed himself to be held.

But these days Sabrina has a whole life outside the Spellman house. When she breezes out, Hilda catches Ambrose's gaze fixed on the door in a way she doesn't like. These days Ambrose doesn't wear rings, or dress as if he might leave the house at any moment.

Perhaps Ambrose is jealous now. Hilda understands the feeling of wanting your own life so much you hate everyone else for having theirs, but Hilda is afraid of the dark passions in other hearts. She didn't know Ambrose was plotting a crime once. She knows, now, that she can never be sure of what Ambrose might do.

If she'd said no to Ambrose more . . . But she can't say no to Ambrose now. She can't say no to Sabrina. All they have to do is look at Hilda and her heart melts, soft as butter in hell.

Zelda says no to Sabrina all the time. Sabrina seldom listens. Hilda worries that is her own fault too. That she really is ruining Sabrina, that Sabrina and Ambrose would both be better off without her.

But she couldn't bear to leave them. Not any of them, even Zelda. Sometimes Hilda has the oddest notion that her sister is even more afraid than she is, and that is why Zelda clings to her and then shoves her away so hard. It makes Hilda want to be gentle, even when Hilda is most frustrated with her. And Hilda wants to be there for Ambrose and Sabrina, to comfort them and stand up for them. That's always been her place.

Death makes you so tired. The earth weighs heavy on her eyelids, sealing them shut. Every time she dies, Hilda feels more tempted to stay in her grave. Living her own life is too hard. Dying her own death might be easier. Hilda could keep her eyes closed, and stay here, be only her own and dream new dreams as tree roots twine through her hair.

My children, Hilda thinks. She opens her eyes, though the earth falls into them and makes them sting. She claws her way upward into the air and the light.

She receives her reward immediately. Sabrina is perched on a nearby gravestone, waiting for Hilda to wake, eating a peach. She swings her Mary Janes against the tombstone. Hilda blinks the grave dirt out of her eyes and watches Sabrina's white teeth sink into the tender flesh of the fruit.

"Why did Aunt Zelda do it?"

Hilda shrugs. Hilda doesn't remember what she said wrong this time, only that she was feeling that itchy, irritable feeling of wanting to be free of Zelda. She snapped at Zelda, and the next thing Hilda knew, her sister was walking toward her with her face white and set, brandishing a knife. There's no sense upsetting Sabrina by discussing the whole ugly business. Hilda just smiles and makes sure Sabrina takes death lightly, and does not consider the consequences.

"No harm done, love."

Sabrina hovers by Hilda's elbow as Hilda makes her way

back into the house. After Hilda is washed up, Ambrose and Sabrina circle around her like attendant birds intent on cheering her. Sabrina is talking about school, Ambrose is telling jokes, making even Zelda rest her chin on her hands and smile. The stove is warm, and the lamps shine behind stained glass. At moments like this, Hilda thinks she has a lovely home and a lovely family. She's very happy here, sometimes.

If Zelda ever struck down Ambrose or Sabrina, no matter if Zelda brought them back the next minute, Hilda thinks she could show the steel and fury people expect of a Spellman. She would know the blood hunger of the tigress in the long grass, whose cubs are under threat. She would pick up the knife or the shovel or the damn axe, and swing.

Who knows what it would do to Sabrina? She is half mortal, half sweet Diana. Hilda never blamed Edward for loving Diana. Hilda loved Diana too. She kept secrets for Diana that nobody knows, and Hilda hopes nobody ever finds out.

Diana died. Mortals are always doing that. But superb, unconquerable Edward died with her. Both Sabrina's parents, mortal and warlock. Maybe there is no way to keep yourself safe from heartbreak.

Nobody has ever heard of a half witch, half mortal before. The Church of Night talks about little else besides Sabrina's coming, Sabrina's dark baptism. The coven hushes when Hilda and Zelda enter. Hilda is so afraid that something might go wrong. She's afraid the world might hurt Sabrina, as it hurt Ambrose, as it destroyed Sabrina's father.

Zelda has never harmed a hair of Ambrose's or Sabrina's heads. Zelda would never do it. Zelda loves the children too, Hilda tells herself. Especially Sabrina, the golden apple of Zelda's eye. Zelda will help Hilda protect Sabrina, and Sabrina will come through her dark baptism and be a shining darkness. Sabrina will make the whole family proud, as Hilda never could.

Hilda ruffles Sabrina's bright hair, resting her arms against the determined line of Sabrina's thin shoulders. She presses her hand against Ambrose's cheek, and he drops a quick kiss in her palm, and she smiles and ignores the grave dirt under her own fingernails.

The fear that wakes her, even in the final darkness beneath the earth, means nothing.

Her children are safe.

THE LAST DAY OF SUMMER

Early the next morning, a truck pulled up outside my house. Ambrose and Aunt Zelda weren't up yet, and I was sitting with Aunt Hilda eating porridge she'd made for me with honey and nuts and hopefully no dried newt eyeballs. Aunt Hilda insists they're nutritious. I find them upsettingly crunchy.

Aunt Hilda was drinking tea with herbs bobbing in her copper mug and reading one of her romance novels. A man with a mullet and a flouncy shirt was on the cover, along with a woman who seemed to be having troubles with her corset and her spine. The romance novel lady couldn't be comfortable, bent over in her hero's arms like that.

"Good book?"

Aunt Hilda beamed. "Oh, Sabrina, it's a gripping read! It's called *Taken by Storm*. The hero's name is Storm."

"That's . . . a wordplay."

I didn't say it was a good one.

"He's also referred to as Satan's minion among the clubs of London," Aunt Hilda continued. "But they're only talking about all his gambling and whoring; he doesn't actually worship the devil. Which was a little disappointing to realize, obviously, but it's still a rattling good yarn! He's a duke, you see, and the heroine is a fishmonger, and she accidentally hits him in the face with a fish. Which gets his attention!"

"I see why it might."

Spiders were playing in Aunt Hilda's hair, spinning cobwebs down to her shoulders and back again like eight-legged trapeze artists. Aunt Hilda's familiars seem to like the romance novels too.

"Finding a priceless ring in the codfish leads him to realize she is the amnesiac assassin who was hired by his greatest enemy! She begins to recover her memories and plot against him, even as Storm is plotting against her. Due to their mutual plotting, they turn from enemies to lovers back to enemies back to lovers again, and their fake engagement turns into an arranged marriage!" Aunt Hilda paused for breath, and beamed. "Also," she added, "Storm is a duke."

"Right. I don't know if their marriage is going to work out."

"Nonsense, Sabrina," said Aunt Hilda. "True love means forgiving each other anything, including assassination attempts. Do you want to read it after I'm finished?"

"I just don't know that the book would live up to the experience of you telling me the story," I told her, which was when I heard the truck.

Hilda and I exchanged a curious look and went to the door together.

It was Harvey. He wore an ecstatic grin as he bounded out of the truck to greet us.

"Hi, Ms. Spellman! Hi, Sabrina! How are you even more beautiful today than yesterday? I wouldn't have thought it was possible, but you make the impossible true every morning! Tommy has a Saturday shift at the mines, and he said he'd drop us off at the fair. My two favorite people both with me. Isn't that the best way to start the day you can imagine?"

Harvey seized me around the waist and rained down light kisses all over my face and hair. I laughed, delighted but a bit embarrassed, and squirmed away.

"Ah, Sabrina's always been as adorable as a sweet little maggot in an apple." Aunt Hilda smiled and waved toward the truck. "Hello, my dear."

She calls all my friends that. Not that Tommy is my friend, but as Harvey's brother I suppose Aunt Hilda figures he's close enough.

Tommy took a hand off the steering wheel and waved back. "Hey, Miz Spellman."

Harvey's brother looked like Harvey, but a less complicated and interesting version. There was nothing of the tortured artist about Tommy. His brow was clear, his voice a calm drawl, and his eyes light blue and laughing while Harvey's were dark and frequently troubled. Not that I didn't like Tommy. I did, even though I didn't know him very well. Everybody liked Tommy. He was famously nice. More important than that, Harvey adored him, worshipped him with the hero worship of a younger brother who had never been disappointed in his idol. That was enough for me.

As I hopped into the back of the truck with Harvey, Tommy gave me his usual friendly smile, and I returned it.

"Maybe I wanted to get a look at the town's latest celebrity," he said. "Harvey couldn't stop talking about you yesterday."

I felt my smile dim. Had he not talked about me before?

"Guess he's looking forward to the fair," Tommy continued.

I forced my smile back into brightness. "I am too."

Harvey linked his fingers together with mine and gave me a shy smile, more like his usual smiles than the wide, sunny smiles of yesterday. I leaned into his side.

"I have a surprise for you," Harvey told me.

I snuggled in. "Yeah?"

"You remember how I stepped in last year to help with the kids getting their faces painted?"

I remembered. Susie and Roz had gone off on their own, and I'd stayed by Harvey's side and pretended it was a date like I wanted it to be.

"The lady at the stall said if I'd take over face-painting duties, then me and my pretty girlfriend"—Harvey squeezed my hand—"could go to the fair for free. We can go on all the rides, play all the games, and even get free cotton candy. Pretty good deal, huh?"

This year, it would be a date. And he'd called me his girlfriend…

Harvey's bright face expected an answer, and it was simple to give him the one he wanted. I cuddled up even closer and whispered: "It's the best. So are you."

The red truck took a sharp curve through the road in the green woods. In the side mirror, I saw Tommy Kinkle's little smile. I wondered if he thought we were dumb kids. My aunts and Ambrose don't take Harvey and me seriously at all. I heard Aunt Zelda say once that many young witches have passing amusements. It wasn't like Edward and Diana, she told Aunt Hilda.

How could she be so sure?

It *was* like Edward and Diana. At least, I hoped it was. I wanted to be like them.

I cleared my throat and said: "I asked my cousin last night where he'd go, if he could go anywhere in the world."

Up front, Tommy huffed a small laugh.

"Sounds like an interesting conversation."

"Yeah," Harvey agreed.

The single word came out small, just as the truck shuddered to a stop outside the fairground. There was a big white sign tied up between two oak trees with the words *LAST DAY OF SUMMER* spelled out on in pasted-on green leaves. Beyond that were throngs of people still dressed for summer in shirtsleeves or short, bright dresses.

I climbed out of the truck, expecting Harvey to follow me. Instead he sat where he was, his head hanging. It was Tommy who jumped out of the driver's seat. We exchanged a concerned look.

"Where would you go, Tommy?" Harvey asked, his voice very low, twisting his hands together. "If you could go anywhere?"

Tommy reached over the side of the truck and grabbed Harvey in a bear hug, resting his forehead against the back of Harvey's neck. I watched as Harvey's melancholy expression brightened into a faint smile, and Tommy closed his laughing blue eyes.

"I'd stay right here with you, Harvey," Tommy murmured back. "You nerd."

There it was, the answer I'd wanted Ambrose to give. I turned away to face the school, ashamed to realize I was jealous. My chest felt uncomfortable, as if there was an animal coiled up around my heart and I could feel it uncurling as it woke.

The sight of them didn't hurt me, but it made me feel in danger of pain, as if the animal wrapped around my heart had claws that might sink in.

Maybe part of growing up is realizing your heart isn't safe.

✳✳✳

The Last Day of Summer fair was set up between Greendale and the neighboring town of Riverdale, though closer to our town, nestled up close to the woods and not too far from the orchard. There were blue-and-white-striped tents set up on a smooth expanse of green grass, and a Ferris wheel in which every carriage was wrought iron, painted white with fancy whorls and crimson velvet seats, like a fairy carriage Cinderella might take to the ball.

The lady who ran the face-painting stall had set us up with stools and a glass bowl full of gumballs, twice as big as marbles and all the colors of the rainbow. She seemed happy to mostly leave Harvey to painting faces while she went off to enjoy the fair with her family.

I perched on a stool, swinging my legs and enjoying the sight of Harvey being extremely adorable with the kids.

He would pick them up and place them gently on a stool so he could reach their faces, then paint with careful tenderness. Sometimes he'd be silent, the tip of his tongue sticking out with concentration as he tried to paint exactly what each kid asked for, and sometimes he would carry on quiet conversations with them, his voice soft and teasing, sounding more like his brother's voice than usual. There was no trace of shyness or hesitation when he talked to kids. Once Harvey was done, he'd take them in his arms and swing them down. The little kids' faces shone with laughter and color.

I wasn't surprised that practically every kid at the fair was lining up.

It did take a while, though, so when one kid needed to be returned to her dad, I went with her. She'd apparently come to the face-painting stall without permission, but her dad didn't really seem mad. I stayed chatting with them until the kid's mom came over with cotton candy for everybody. I thought wistfully that the little girl was lucky to have such nice parents.

I strolled out on my own beneath the shadow of the Ferris wheel, studying the red tie around my wrist that let me enter all the rides and attractions for free. Harvey had touched the tie proudly and suggested I go to the Hall of Mirrors on my own.

The Hall of Mirrors was a barn painted black, with silver threads of tinsel hanging through the open doors. I showed my wristband to a bored-looking boy about my own age, who was wearing a hat and texting furiously.

Inside were hay bales draped with black cloth and twisting passageways lined with mirrors. I could hear other people in the distance, giggling and shrieking and lost. I wandered through the maze, whistling. When you have twisting tree branches in your walls and dead people in your basement, I guess you grow up harder to impress.

Then I came to a dead end. A large, murky mirror was hanging in my path, blocking the way. The surface of the mirror seemed almost wavy as well as dark, like lake water ruffled by a night wind. There was only one light to be found reflected in the mirror, a flash of intense brightness like something burning far away. I moved nearer.

When I realized the pale, burning light was my face, I stopped dead, unsettled by the face I hadn't recognized, that was and yet was not mine.

The Hall of Mirrors was dark, but there must be sunshine creeping in through chinks. Rays of light pierced through the loose waves of my hair. My face in the mirror was indistinct; I could not make it out no matter how close I came, but I could see how it shone.

It made me recall, with sudden violent clarity, the words of the spirit by the stream.

The moon shone behind you like a crown of bone, and the night streamed behind you like a cloak of shadows. I could see you were born to be a witch of legend.

I should go talk to the wishing-well spirit again, I thought. She'd wanted me to. *I* wanted to go. I felt the urge with the same irresistible force as I'd remembered the words. It was pulling me to leave the fairground, abandon Harvey, and walk deep into the woods this moment.

But that was ridiculous. I wouldn't leave Harvey to go anywhere. And besides, I realized, I wasn't entirely certain how to get out of the maze of mirrors. Somehow I'd gotten as turned around and lost as any mortal.

But witches don't stay lost.

I took a little spool of thread out of my pocket (the one I always carry because Aunt Hilda insists), dropped it on the ground, and watched it roll by itself across the earth floor.

"Consequitur quodcunque petit," I murmured: a little spell I've always liked. It means *She attains whatever she seeks.*

Take that, Ambrose. My Latin was perfect. He'd been speaking too fast; that was why I hadn't understood him.

Almost as if he hadn't wanted me to hear the spell.

I shook off the moment of doubt and followed the thread, walking confidently through the maze of mirrors.

I came out through the shivering silver doorway and saw one of my teachers standing in the shadow of the Ferris wheel.

She was dressed in her usual blouse and tweed skirt, as if she was still in school rather than on a day off.

"Hi, Ms. Wardwell!"

She gave me a timid smile, blinking behind her large glasses as if startled to be recognized. "Hello, Sabrina."

"Here with anyone?"

"Oh—no," said Ms. Wardwell. "I just came to see the fair. This is the hundredth Last Day of Summer fair; that's rather momentous, isn't it?" She patted her brown bun, and more wisps came loose around her hairpins. "Nobody but me seems to realize. I'm by way of being Greendale's unofficial historian."

"That's cool," I told her encouragingly.

It was slightly weird to feel protective of one of your teachers, but Ms. Wardwell always seemed to be shrinking away from the world, sweet and easily frightened as a small brown field mouse.

"Why, thank you, Sabrina," said Ms. Wardwell, and added after a moment of hesitation: "It's nice to see all the families here, having such a good time."

I hesitated, glancing back to the stall where Harvey seemed to be wrapping up, and sent him a tiny smile. By the time I turned back to Ms. Wardwell, she was giving me an embarrassed nod.

"Well, nice to see you, my dear."

"Wait—"

She wandered off, the kitten heels on her sensible brown shoes sinking into the earth. I was alone once more under the Ferris wheel, feeling a little sorry for both Ms. Wardwell and myself. I hadn't realized our teacher was actually lonely.

Then, as the evening closed in, the lights of the Ferris wheel came on. I'd been expecting the little yellow bulbs around the swinging carriages to flicker on, but I hadn't expected the shimmering projections in the air: bluebirds and butterflies and stars and hearts and flowers, as if someone had collected illustrations from a hundred love stories and was tossing them up in the air like confetti.

If there was any witch but me around, I'd have thought it was magic.

A few moments later, I realized what must be going on. I remembered what Ms. Wardwell had said. People were pulling out all the stops for the hundredth anniversary of the Last Day of Summer.

My guess was proved correct when the fireworks started.

I tipped my head back admiringly, and smiled, and realized I wasn't on my own anymore. Harvey was beside me. His face was slightly dazed, and he was adjusting his flannel shirt, but when he saw my smile, he smiled too.

"Long day painting faces?" I asked. "My artistic hero. What do you say we go on the Ferris wheel?"

"I would follow you to hell," declared Harvey.

"Not necessary," I assured him. "The Ferris wheel seems like it would be fun."

Harvey took my hand in a courtly gesture and helped me into the carriage of the Ferris wheel with a bow, like a knight out of a fairy tale. "My lady."

"Get in here, fool," I said, and pulled him down onto the red velvet seat with me.

The Ferris wheel swung forward with a jolt, the carriage swinging slightly in the air. As we rose, I kicked out my feet over the fairground turning small beneath me. The miles of green woods turned black as night fell, and I imagined how it might feel to fly.

Then I turned to look into Harvey's eyes. He was watching me, not the skies, with his most attentive and serious gaze, the way he only looks at what he wants to draw and finds beautiful. I wanted him to keep looking at me exactly that way just as much as I wanted to fly.

"Sabrina," Harvey murmured, "I lo—"

I kissed him to cut him off, my fingers twining tight in his hair. I desperately wanted to hear it, and I desperately didn't. I wanted it to be real.

That was as ridiculous as a witch getting lost in a barn. A little tiny spell didn't mean this wasn't real.

When the desperate kiss was over, Harvey said, "Wow," soft and pleased, eyes lowered, the shadow of his lashes dark on his cheeks.

I smoothed his hair, gone wildly ruffled where I had grabbed at him, putting everything to rights. I hadn't done Harvey any harm. I would never hurt him, and even if I'd done this without his permission or knowledge, like Aunt Hilda said: *True love means forgiving each other anything.* I'd always had to keep secrets from him. This was just one more.

There were still fireworks going off in the sky. Though the fairground and the woods were slipping into shadow, Catherine wheels and Roman candles illuminated the night. There were green fireworks whose light traced sinuous paths over the night sky like snakes. There were fireworks that gleamed the electric blue of kingfishers. There were fireworks like the lights of falling stars, glittering so fiercely they left the remnants of their light scattered like gold dust in Harvey's lowered lashes.

Our carriage swayed, high above the night and wrapped in light. Then he leaned in, so slowly, to kiss me again.

It was easy to believe that there was no magic tonight, except for this.

WHAT HAPPENS IN THE DARK

A witch's day out is not like a mortal day out. A witch is more likely to be out at night, sky-clad or kissing the moon.

Harvey didn't know this, or that his girlfriend was a witch, or that witches were real. He'd been planning to take Sabrina to the fair for months. They had gone last year, and Harvey had painted some kids' faces just for fun, and the kids had gone wild for it. Mrs. Grabeel had kindly offered that if he came back and did it again officially this year, he and his girlfriend could ride all the rides and play all the games for free.

It was the best deal Harvey had ever heard. He didn't have a lot of money to take Sabrina out.

He used to worry about that. Right now, he couldn't

imagine why. Right now, he couldn't imagine worrying about anything at all. The world was such a beautiful place.

It was such a beautiful day. Harvey tried to train himself to have an artist's eye, appreciating every detail, and there was a lot to appreciate. The white Ferris wheel spun against the background of trees, like a lace doily turning on a table. There were clouds blanketing the sky, but even the clouds were drenched in sunshine, so that everywhere Harvey looked was a picture framed in hazy gold.

Masses of people had turned up for the festival. There were even strangers here in Greendale, Harvey marveled: A woman with a cool lavender mohawk enthusiastically buying funnel cake. A boy in black who looked like a preppy Goth with a hair-gel addiction, eyeing his toffee apple with mingled hostility and suspicion. A man in an expensive business suit, who brought both his little girls to the stall to get their faces painted.

And the most marvelous person at the fair was there in the stall with Harvey. Sabrina was handing him his paints.

"You can go ahead and get on the rides," Harvey said proudly. "It's my treat."

"I'll wait to go on them with you," Sabrina told him, tucking her hand briefly into the curve of his elbow.

Her touch went through him like light through water, making anything that had been dark suddenly clear.

"I'll try not to be too long," Harvey promised. "If you get bored, you can always try the Hall of Mirrors. I got lost in there when I was a kid, and I'm not going back."

There had been so many mirrors, showing so many Harveys. In the silvery dark of the mirrors, he'd felt as if he was seeing a thousand different weak, pathetic versions of his soul, felt as if he was looking through his father's eyes at himself. In every mirror, his eyes were scared.

Harvey had collapsed with a whimper. Tommy had charged in and led him out. That was like Tommy, Harvey thought. He wasn't sure why he'd been scared at all. He should have known Tommy would always come for him.

He couldn't imagine being worried or scared today, but he still didn't want to go into that hall of mirrors and shadows. He didn't want to look at any version of himself. He only wanted to look at Sabrina.

She was a bright constant at the edge of his vision as Harvey chewed on the gumballs big as marbles that Mrs. Grabeel had left in the stall and busily painted all the kids' faces. There was an enormous line at the face-painting stall, and Harvey was pretty pleased with himself. He'd always gotten along with kids: He'd heard somebody say that he was nonthreatening. They hadn't meant it as a compliment, but Harvey had taken it as one. Who wanted to be threatening?

Harvey knew how it felt to be afraid of someone big and

angry. He'd never want to make kids feel that way. It was far better to make them smile.

When the line was almost at an end, Harvey painted, on request, green and blue butterflies all over the face of one very little girl in a pink tulle skirt. The pièce de résistance was a big purple butterfly, its wings spread over the bridge of her nose.

"I can't see my dad," the little girl said, her brow slightly furrowed.

"Don't you fret," Harvey told her. "My beautiful assistant and I will find him."

Harvey showed the little girl her butterflies in the round looking glass, and she giggled and lifted her hands out to him. He picked her up off the stool and twirled her around, her ballerina skirt a frilly blur, and gave her a kiss on the tip of the nose before he put her in Sabrina's arms. Sabrina folded the little girl against her, the child's chubby hands clutching on to Sabrina's pretty green sweater.

Sabrina wrinkled her own adorable nose at the kid, and as the little girl laughed Harvey could almost imagine the iridescent wings of the butterflies were quivering, about to take flight. He laughed with her, and Sabrina joined them, and for a moment they were all laughing with their arms around each other in a circle of spinning color.

Even the surly boy in black paused as he went by the stall, sharp, dark eyes narrowing slightly as he studied the painted butterflies.

Harvey scanned the fairground and located the man in the expensive business suit, hand in hand with his older daughter. Harvey thought, with his new sense of expansive goodwill, that the man must be a great dad. His kids didn't seem scared of him at all.

"Could you take Miss Butterflies to her dad, Sabrina?"

"No problem," agreed Sabrina, the sweetest girl in the world.

"Another kiss," chirped the little kid.

Harvey grinned and dropped another kiss on her tiny nose. Since he was down there, he kissed Sabrina's nose too, and got to see the kindling spark of her smile up close.

When he surfaced Harvey saw that the guy in black was still watching, and he was smiling a little smile too. Sabrina walked away, carrying the kid toward the Ferris wheel.

Normally Harvey would have been shy with a stranger, and definitely with someone like this, a guy his own age with that indefinable but unmistakable air of cool that everyone at school could recognize you had or you didn't. The guy had on a long black coat that looked *tailored*. Harvey was wearing his brother's battered sheepskin-lined jacket.

At any other time, that would have mattered. Today the world was golden, and it seemed easy to smile casually at the other guy and say: "So cute, right?".

If Harvey meant Sabrina's shining head bent tenderly over the child more than anything else, nobody had to know that.

The guy in black seemed vaguely startled to be addressed, but before unease could lance Harvey's glowing bubble of courage, the brief moment of hesitation was over and the boy's smile spread.

"Yeah, actually," he answered. "Very cute."

After another pause, which seemed contemplative, the boy seemed to come to a decision and swung himself over the side into the stall. Harvey stared, then glanced nervously over at Mrs. Grabeel, who was passing out pinwheels to kids waiting for their faces to be painted.

"You're not really allowed—" Harvey began.

The boy made a dismissive gesture. "Mortal rules don't apply to me."

Harvey said blankly: "What?".

Mrs. Grabeel glanced over her shoulder, and the boy directed his smile at her. Mrs. Grabeel actually simpered and patted her hair.

"Oh, it's fine for any friend of yours to keep you company, Harvey. You're doing a great job!"

Harvey beamed reflexively, thrilled she thought so, and Mrs. Grabeel had already turned back to her task before Harvey thought to protest: "But I don't, um, know him at all…?"

"Nick," said the boy. "Carry on."

Nick, Harvey thought, did not understand boundaries. He'd grabbed a stool and was leafing through the sketches Harvey had made to give the kids ideas for how they'd like their faces painted, scattering the pages carelessly around.

"You gave that girl butterflies."

"That was what she asked for," said Harvey.

Nick glanced up from the pages, firing another smile. Harvey wasn't sure if this was an entirely nice smile. Nick seemed amused, and Harvey knew what mean jokes felt like, jokes he wasn't meant to be part of.

"Not much for double entendres, are we? Or single entendres."

Harvey shrugged uncomfortably. He kind of wished Nick would leave. This day was so bright, and the boy was the only dark blot on the golden landscape.

The next little kid tugged on Harvey's sleeve. "Want to be a dinosaur."

"Oh, like a fierce dinosaur? Like a *Tyrannosaurus rex*?" Harvey made a *Tyrannosaurus rex* sound.

"Except I don't want to go 'xtinct!"

"No way," said Harvey. "Anyway, maybe the dinosaurs didn't go extinct. They say maybe the dinosaurs turned into birds."

"No!" The kid laughed. "Birds don't look like dinosaurs."

Harvey carefully painted the chomping teeth of a *Tyrannosaurus rex* around the kid's mouth. "Some do. In Australia, there's a bird called a cassowary. I've read about them. Some of them grow to be six feet tall, and they have really sharp claws."

Harvey made a pretend swipe with his claws at the kid, and the kid squirmed, thrilled, and pranced off to display his dinosaur face to his mom. Nick was giving Harvey an odd look, probably thinking about how much of a loser Harvey was. That was certainly what people thought in school.

Nobody had invited Nick to the face-painting stall.

"It's true about cassowaries," Harvey said defensively. "There's a lot more cool stuff in the world than people realize."

"Oh, I'm sure. *There are more things in hell and earth, Horatio, than are dreamt of in your philosophy*," Nick murmured.

Harvey blinked. "*Heaven and earth*. That's the quote. Shakespeare, right? *There are more things in heaven and earth . . .*"

"If you say so." Nick wore the beginnings of that mocking smile again. "I really wouldn't know."

Harvey would usually have been afraid to say what he was thinking, but these past few days there had been no fear. Heedless grand thoughts kept spilling out of his mouth with none of the usual doubts stopping him, and he could not stop the flood now.

"There are cassowaries. The northern lights sometimes shine red and blue as well as green. And there are fish that glow neon, and all those things are real. There are amazing sights in the world, things that seem like miracles and sound like stories, but they're true, and while you're waiting to see marvels, there are the miracles at home that remind you they're true." Harvey stopped talking, felt past the luminous confidence that he must have sounded incredibly foolish, and muttered: "You know what I mean?"

Nick was shaking his dark head emphatically.

"No. Not at all."

Harvey felt even more like a total idiot.

Nick hesitated, a longer pause than any before. Then he said, in a soft voice: "But it sounds nice."

Harvey nodded, encouraged. "Yeah. You know how sometimes, things hurt so much, and you can't figure out why, and you don't know how to put all the pieces together so they make sense?"

Nick bit his lip. "I do try to work things out a lot. I don't . . . always succeed."

"I hardly ever do," said Harvey honestly. "But sometimes I walk into school, and I see a girl, and suddenly everything that was murky goes crystal clear. Or I go into my house and I think something bad might happen, but I see my brother instead. Or I walk through the woods, and up to a girl's house, and the door opens, and it doesn't matter if there is fog or rain. Everything makes perfect sense. Everything shines."

Harvey was silent for an instant, thinking about his brother. There was something he'd been really concerned about, but he couldn't seem to hold on to any worries. He tried hard for a moment, so hard his head hurt with the effort, and still he couldn't remember.

Nick's voice was questing away from softness, where he'd seemed somewhat lost, and back to cynicism. "Oh, a girl?"

"*The* girl," corrected Harvey.

"There are a lot of girls," Nick remarked. "I wouldn't want to limit myself if I were you. In fact, if we're talking about the marvels this world has to offer, the world is filled with a great many very attractive—"

"Not like this one," Harvey said, positive. "Not a girl who changes the world. Love makes the world make sense. You'd have to be an idiot not to want the key to every secret in the universe."

"So you like her because she'll give you all the answers?"

"She is all the answers," said Harvey. "It's not about what she gives me."

A little boy tugged sharply on Harvey's loose, worn jeans. He had the expression of someone who might have been waiting for some time while a loser made a weird, impassioned speech about love.

"Sorry!" Harvey was mortified. "What would you like?"

The kid cheered up at once. "Tiger!"

Harvey began to paint a tiger on the kid's face, a big splash of orange and bold strokes of black.

"Wow, okay. Hey, mortal, do you normally talk to strangers like this?" Nick asked faintly, but the hard edge was gone from his voice again.

"No," said Harvey, absentmindedly. "I get nervous talking to strangers."

"You could have fooled me!" Nick exclaimed. "I mean, launching into deep philosophical conversations about, like, feelings . . . I normally just have sex with people, or curse them, you know, normal stuff . . ."

Harvey was focused on painting a tiger face and not really paying attention, but he did register that this bizarre boy had just said the word *sex* in front of *a kid*. He shot Nick a scandalized glare.

"What?" Nick said. He was looking somewhat shaken. "I mean, it's fine. It's good. I like it. I think. It's just you don't understand. There are people who have hearts as hard and cold as the highest stone wall."

"Sorry," Harvey said. "But that's garbage. Hearts aren't walls. You might build walls around your heart because you don't want to be hurt, but that seems really sad. It would mean not feeling anything at all."

Nick bit his lip. "I've had . . . feelings? Not recently. But in my life. I've had—some feelings? I'm capable of talking about feelings."

He looked away and carefully began to straighten all the sketches that he'd messed up. Harvey was appeased. It was difficult to hold on to any negative thoughts, the way he was feeling right now. Shock or worry, fears or doubts, they slid off the shining surface of Harvey's mind. He put the last touches on the tiger, which was turning out well, and began to hum under his breath.

"You seem . . . really happy," Nick ventured, sounding lost again.

Harvey said: "I am."

He stepped back and showed the kid his tiger face. Behind him, he heard Nick murmur something he didn't catch.

The sunlight hit the mirror. The tiger face was even better than Harvey had thought. It seemed so real that for a moment, Harvey could have sworn he saw the painted whiskers twitch.

The kid's face split into an incredulous grin. Harvey grinned back at him and made a little roaring noise. As he put the mirror down, the glass caught Nick's reflection too, winking at the kid and smiling secretly to himself. That smile wasn't mean at all. Maybe none of them had been, Harvey thought, with that new all-encompassing feeling of warmth for everybody in the world.

Harvey never wanted to be fearful or suspicious, not of anyone. He just hadn't been able to help it. But now, suddenly, he could do better.

Maybe Nick was just lonely, or unhappy. Harvey tilted the mirror and flashed him a bright smile in return.

Nick seemed distinctly pleased. "These sketches are pretty good. Do you draw a lot?"

"Often as I can." Harvey was taken aback but gratified by the sudden interest. "When my dad isn't watching."

Nick's nod was approving. "I like a rebel."

"Do you draw?"

"Not like this. Sigils for rituals, that sort of thing. For school," Nick explained. "For the advanced classes."

"Oh, the *advanced* classes," said Harvey. "Nerd."

It occurred to him as soon as he said it that this was not a great thing to say to someone you had just met. Tommy often called Harvey that, and Harvey liked it. The word sounded soft in Tommy's mouth, affectionate. Harvey hoped the word hadn't sounded harsh in his own mouth.

He didn't think it had.

Nick was running his hand through his almost-black hair, still smiling. "Whatever, farm boy."

Harvey didn't have any friends who were guys, and didn't

really have any experience in what was okay to say to them or not. Most guys in school sneered at Harvey for liking art, only having friends who were girls, and not wanting to talk about football. Harvey always had the uneasy feeling that whatever flaw his dad saw in him, the guys at school could sense too.

It would be nice, he thought with sudden hope, to have a friend who was a guy.

"Do you like football?" Harvey asked.

Nick blinked. "What's football?"

Harvey grinned. "That's how I feel about football as well."

The line of kids that had seemed endless was at an end, and all over the fairground there were children with pretty designs or fantastical paintings on their faces. The kids were brightening up the fair, and Harvey thought he might have brightened up their day. That was all Harvey wanted, to add a little light to the world. The sky was getting darker, but that meant the horizon was a line of pure gold.

It was as though every shadow of fear or doubt had been stripped from Harvey's eyes, and whatever he saw shone.

Sabrina was talking to one of their teachers by the Ferris wheel. Shadows had leaped from leaf to leaf until they turned the trees entirely dark, but the Ferris wheel was a delicate circle of lights. They gleamed on Sabrina's shining bob, dancing at her ears in the slight breeze, interrupted by the tiny darkness of her hairband. He saw her sneak a look over at the stall and note that the line was gone. In profile, he saw the curve of her oddly wise smile. She knew he'd be coming to her soon.

"That's her," Harvey told Nick. "The only girl in the world. That's Sabrina. Isn't she the most beautiful thing under heaven?"

Nick's voice scraped a little. "Oh, hell yes." He drummed his fingers restlessly on the side of the stall. "So that's the famous Sabrina. I thought it might be."

Harvey frowned, puzzled, but then he was distracted by the flare of sudden lights. The little girl with the butterflies painted on her face got into one of the carriages on the Ferris wheel with her sister. As the carriage jolted into motion, colored lights bloomed around it, creating the shape of a butterfly with its wings outstretched. The wings dissolved into a ruby-red rose, soft petals unfurling.

The shimmering reflection fell on Sabrina, as if she was being picked out by a spotlight, her smooth hair dyed deep, sudden crimson. The rose became the first star of evening, seven crystalline points spinning as the Ferris wheel did, and Sabrina's gold hair was now snow white. Harvey drew in a deep, wondering breath and fumbled for his pencils. Things like that sometimes happened around Sabrina, as though she changed the world just by moving through it. His magic girl.

He reached for the paper, and as he did so his gaze fell on Nick, whose hand was lifted as if framing the star between his fingers. Nick's eyes were wide, the darkness of them filled with dazzling white light.

On the soft exhalation of his wondering breath, Harvey said: "How lovely. It's just like magic."

He set his pencil to paper and drew Sabrina under the Ferris wheel, focused on the movement of the colored point across the blank page, turning what had been nothing into a reflection of beauty.

"So . . ." Nick cleared his throat. "Are you down to share?"

"What?" Harvey realized what Nick was asking and pushed the glass bowl of gumballs in Nick's direction with his free hand. "Sure."

Nick took a gumball with a slow, pleased smile. "That's great."

Over the fairground, where the dome of the sky was deep blue, descending into green, copper, and the final line of gold, fireworks bloomed sudden and silent as flowers in shadow. Streaks of brilliant red cut through the dark like bleeding stars.

Harvey said, thrilled: "Oh my God."

"He doesn't have anything to do with it," Nick muttered. "I don't see why he should be getting the praise."

Harvey was distracted by the dazzling array of colors, the delicate curves of daffodil yellow and white clusters of baby's breath and bright blue dots of forget-me-nots joining the rose red, the looping lines of leafy green. It was as if the night sky was a dark stranger that had come carrying a bouquet of lights.

"Nothing like this happened at the fair last year," said Harvey. "This is amazing." He became aware that even in the dark woods there were flowers blooming, their colors sudden and dazzling. He couldn't believe he hadn't noticed them before.

"You're drawing a picture. You like it." Nick sounded glad. "But that's nothing. I can—I bet the whole Ferris wheel could just come loose and roll around the whole fairground and light it all up."

Harvey stopped drawing the picture.

"If the Ferris wheel came loose and rolled around the fairground, then—"

Nick's expression was eager. For some reason, he'd rolled up his sleeves. "It would be exciting and artistic?"

"People would be crushed and killed. That would be—"

Nick made a face. "Messy?"

"A horrible tragedy!"

"Oh, right," said Nick. He began to roll down his sleeves with a disappointed air. "Lucky it won't happen, then."

Harvey nodded, briefly appalled by Nick's morbid imagination. The twinge of unease passed like every other worry was passing these days: as if swiftly erased by a hand drawing the story of his life, not allowing for any unharmonious mistakes. Nick might be like Sabrina, who loved horror movies with a deep and inexplicable passion. Harvey brightened at the thought.

"Do you want to come meet Sabrina with me?" he asked.

Nick's face lit up momentarily. "I'd like that very much. Let me think about it for a minute."

Harvey nodded. "No rush." He shoved pencils, paints, and papers into his bag, still thinking happily of horror movies and potential double dates. He'd often thought that it would be great to find someone smart and nice for Roz. Harvey realized that given what he'd seen of Nick's personality thus far, Roz's dad would probably *not* like Nick, but maybe that didn't matter.

"Hey, are you single?"

"I can be," Nick said easily. "If it matters."

Harvey frowned. "What does that mean?"

Nick made a soothing sound, as if hushing a cry. "Don't worry about it. Sabrina is waiting for you."

Her name woke a memory. Harvey felt suspicion rise in him, and then the suspicion almost slipped through his fingers again, as he felt the almost overwhelming urge to stop worrying and be happy. This time he thought of Sabrina, and managed to hold on.

"You said," Harvey told Nick slowly. "You said *So that's the famous Sabrina*. What did you mean by that? What's going on?"

"Don't be mad," said Nick. "It's not *my* fault you don't know anything."

"What the hell are you talking about?"

His voice was sharp in his own ears, like a warning telling Harvey that he should be afraid. The stall was a small wooden cage full of shadows. Nick rose from the stool, and it shouldn't have been menacing, Harvey was taller than Nick, but it was. Nick moved forward in a purposeful prowl, and Harvey jolted back. It was as though a mask had fallen from Nick's face, his eyes doorways into darkness, and Harvey was struck with horror at the realization of how stupid he had been. This was no friend. Harvey thought, with cold, creeping certainty: This was an ancient enemy.

"And this looked like it would be such a fun night too," Nick murmured, sounding mildly regretful. There was no light left in his eyes. "But no, now is not the time. Seems like a whole lot of drama amid the cotton candy. I don't want to make a bad first impression."

Smoke from the fireworks seemed to be filtering through the air, making Harvey's mouth dry. "I don't understand."

"You will, farm boy," promised Nick. "But not tonight. Forget."

"Sorry?" Harvey asked, stunned. As if he could.

Nick nodded. "I am, a little. This is meant to be a blessing, but—what a shame for you—I'm not really the blessing type.

Blind your mind and blind your heart
Let these painful thoughts depart."

"Wait—" Harvey said desperately.

Nick blew him a kiss and dropped him a wink. Nick's dark amusement was the last thing Harvey saw before a blanket seemed to fall on his struggling thoughts, smoothing everything out, muffling his senses.

"What were you going to do before you met me?"

He was right there, but Nick's voice, almost idly curious, seemed on the cusp of hearing. He was slipping out of sight somehow.

Harvey blinked hard as his vision blurred. "Go on the Ferris wheel with Sabrina—tell her I love her—I've never told her—"

"Oh." Nick's voice was soft. "Seems like you should do that, then."

Harvey nodded in a quick, jerky motion, a puppet manipulated by careless hands. The searching, bewildered look faded from his face. He stumbled away from the stall, his steps faltering at first but then growing surer as he walked toward Sabrina.

"See you later," murmured Nicholas Scratch. He moved farther from the light and out of memory, grinning a sharp, wicked grin and chewing his gum.

A witch's day out can turn dangerous.

THE WEIRD SISTERS

he Last Day of Summer fair ended beautifully, and the rest of the weekend was nice. I went out for coffee with Roz and Susie, and when I came home Ambrose opened the door for me and Aunt Hilda was making Aunt Zelda's favorite dinner. Everybody seemed entirely cheerful, not at all as if Ambrose was keeping secrets from me or Aunt Zelda had killed Aunt Hilda a few days ago.

I tried not to think about any of it, and I was mostly successful.

On Monday I came downstairs to find Ambrose flirting with the lady who delivered the mail again. He was wearing jeans and a real T-shirt he hadn't slept in, so he probably liked her. He gave me an unusually bright smile and an enthusiastic wave as I came down our split-level staircase.

"Hello, cousin!"

"*Is* she your cousin?" asked the mailwoman.

"That is why I call her that, yes," said Ambrose. "Seems like an odd nickname."

"I just meant—" She blushed one of those easy, deep redhead blushes, a red tide rushing to drown her freckles. "Since you're African American."

I came to stand at Ambrose's elbow and eat my cereal at her with concentrated hostility. "What do you mean by that? So he can't be my cousin?"

"I didn't mean that," she said.

I finished my cereal and grasped hold of Ambrose's elbow, holding on tight. Ambrose nudged me away gently.

"It is pretty ridiculous," he said. "I'm not African American. I'm *British*. There is a Union Jack in my bedroom. Which you won't be seeing."

That was what he was upset about? I stared while the mailwoman made her escape, glaring at both of us. I thought we might have a lot of things lost in the mail for the next few weeks—until Aunt Zelda rerouted the mail delivery again.

Ambrose wandered over to the windows. I wondered if he was watching the woman leave, but when I came closer I saw his face was tipped up to the sky, his eyes narrowed. He lifted a hand, finger and thumb tracing the path of birds flying through the air.

"How are you feeling?" I asked.

"If I'm ever allowed to have a familiar again," Ambrose said, "I might want a bird."

A witch's familiar is a goblin in animal form who is their partner in all magic. Aunt Hilda has her spiders. Sometimes when she reads her romance novels she sits at the kitchen table with the spiders crawling in a black stream up her wrist to sit in the hollow of her free hand, held up to the pages as if their eight eyes are reading about stormy, romantic adventures too. For my dark baptism, I'll be getting a familiar of my own. Aunt Zelda has already left a few helpful pedigree books around the place, marked and highlighted, but I haven't decided what kind of familiar I want yet.

Still, I'm excited about it. A familiar will be like another member of the family, someone who will always take my side and never leave me and understand everything about magic. A familiar is a witch's constant companion.

According to the terms of his sentence, Ambrose is forbidden to have a familiar.

I rested my cheek against his shoulder. "What kind of bird?"

"Oh, I don't know, cousin, I'm just talking. I'd be happy with any kind of familiar. I'm this close to painting a smiley face on a rock."

He shrugged me airily off, moving toward an earthenware vase on a side table. He lifted it in his hands and mimicked a squeaky voice.

"Hello, Sabrina. I'm Ambrose's new familiar. Together we will make powerful magic!"

I giggled. "Might not be quite up to Aunt Z.'s standards."

"Well, if I ever do get a familiar again, Auntie Z. certainly isn't going to be picking one out for me." Ambrose put his vase back down on the table. "I don't want a creature bred in captivity. I know how that feels too well. I'm taking no prisoners."

I nodded. "That makes sense."

I hadn't thought about it before, but that made a *lot* of sense. Maybe soon, very soon now, when it was my turn to get a familiar, I'd want one who was wild too. A familiar who would choose to stay with me.

Ambrose was staring out the window again. The last swallows of summer were zigging and zagging across the sky, the delicate arches of their black wings cutting dark lines that almost resembled the lines on a map.

"Maybe a bird," he murmured.

I keep forgetting that if Ambrose could choose, he wouldn't be here with me.

"What did your spell say?"

I didn't realize how sharp the question came out until I saw Ambrose's eyes narrow.

"Oh, not this again," he said. "I'm not talking about this! I don't talk about anything that bores me."

"But—"

Ambrose pointed a finger and then whirled toward the door when a knock came. He flung the door dramatically open, all while still pointing at me. "I said no! No to boredom. I'm off to the mortuary, where all the exciting conversationalists are! *'The crack in the tea-cup opens/A lane to the land of the dead!'* Right about now." He exited through the arched door under the stairs. I might have followed him except that Harvey and, oddly, his brother, Tommy, were standing in the doorway. They looked understandably perplexed.

"Hi?" said Tommy.

"Are you sure you should be bringing teacups down to the morgue?" asked Harvey.

They were both answered only by Ambrose slamming the door. I went over and patted Harvey's arm. My man, asking the real questions.

"Ha-ha," I said. "Ignore him, Harvey. Hey, Tommy. Fancy seeing you twice in one week!"

Tommy shrugged easily. "I have early shifts for the next few days, so I figured I could take you and Harvey to school."

"You work too much. You should take better care of yourself," Harvey said, his brow clouded for a moment. Then he looked at me, and it cleared. "And you should just stay perfect."

I popped up on my toes to give him a quick kiss. "I'll try."

We climbed into Tommy's red pickup truck and made for Baxter High.

"Funny guy, your cousin," Tommy remarked.

I bristled. First the mailwoman, and now this. "How do you mean?"

Tommy sounded taken aback. "I mean—he made a joke? About dead people being exciting conversationalists?"

I deflated. "Oh."

"Like I said, funny."

"Yeah," I muttered. "He's a scream. That was a quote, by the way, about the teacup and the land of the dead, not demented babbling. It's from a poem by W. H. Auden."

Tommy raised his eyebrows at Harvey in the sideview mirror.

"Smart girl you've got there. Family who quotes poetry to each other. Hang on to that one."

"That's my plan," said Harvey, his arm around my shoulders.

I had my arm around his waist. I didn't want to let go either.

At school, Tommy leaned out of the window to give Harvey a hug goodbye. The two of them held on for a moment, casually affectionate, really sure of each other. Really family.

"Take care of yourself down there," said Harvey.

Tommy winked at me over his brother's shoulder. "Take care of him, Sabrina."

Harvey slid his arm back around me as we went up the stairs and into the hallway, where the glass in the windows made the light filtering through faintly green, as if we were underwater. Ms. Wardwell gave me a tiny smile as she scuttled past, but she didn't stay to talk.

There was a line drawn between Harvey's brows. "I hate thinking about him down there. I hate those stupid mines."

"I'm sorry."

Harvey looked at me as I spoke, and the line between his brows softened. "You're beautiful," he said. "Like a star I can't believe I get to keep."

Susie came over to us and headbutted him in the shoulder. "Chill out, Romeo."

Harvey blinked at her, puzzled. "But nothing's more important than true love."

"Sure there is," said Roz, coming to my side. "Consider your GPA."

"Ease up on Harvey," I begged when we were in the girls' bathroom, washing my hands clean. "He's not being that weird."

"He is!" Susie and Roz both yelled from their respective stalls. "He is being THAT weird."

I scrubbed at my hands with renewed vigor. The pale pink soap from the dispensers was turning an unpleasant color, like foam flecked with blood. Your hands can never be too clean.

"You don't understand," I said in a low voice.

Roz came out and joined me, tilting her head at her reflection in the mirror. There was something odd about the way she was staring at herself. She was squinting too much.

"What don't we understand?"

"It's nothing, it's fine," I told her. "How's your head?"

Roz swung her head toward me. For a moment, her gaze looked unfocused, as if she couldn't think what I meant.

"Your head was hurting," I prompted her.

"It was nothing," she murmured. "It's fine."

I couldn't say: *I'm a half witch, and on my next birthday, in little more than a month, I will go through my dark baptism and become a full witch. My family want me to do it, and I want to do magic, but I'm pretty sure my family expect me to leave my whole mortal life, including you guys, in the dust. I'm holding on as hard as I can to Harvey and to you, but I'm not sure what to do. And that's new for me. I'm used to being sure.*

Susie came out of her own stall, washing her hands while studiously avoiding her reflection. I stared at them both hopelessly.

They wouldn't understand. I couldn't tell them, and I couldn't talk to my aunts or Ambrose about Harvey, not really. There was nobody in the world I could talk to about everything.

I wished for my parents. Then I thought about the spirit of the wishing well.

✳✳✳

"Actually," I said when Harvey was walking me home on the path through the woods, "you can leave me here. I was thinking I might like to take a walk through the woods. Okay, bye!"

I gave him a breezy wave and began to power walk through the trees. Seconds later, I heard him crashing after me. There was no way, barring magic, that I was outpacing him. My legs are short, like the rest of me.

When he caught up with me, Harvey was beaming. "I'll come with you!"

"You'll be bored," I said desperately. "I am going to collect, uh, flowers. And press them in a book. Then I will have many dried flowers."

"Flowers for the rose of the world." Harvey smiled. "I'd like to draw you collecting flowers. Nothing you do could be boring."

I made an impatient gesture. "See, nobody is fascinating one hundred percent of the time. People sleep. People go to the bathroom. Nobody's fascinating in the bathroom."

Harvey seemed bewildered. "Well . . . I'm sure you're . . ."

"Actually, I don't want to pursue this line of discussion!" I told him quickly. "I'd like us to stay together and not be mentally scarred for life. Sure, let's go."

We walked hand in hand through the woods, under the dappled sunlight and the shadow of the leaves. Until I spied what I was searching for: the tiny scarlet flash of a ladybug curled up in a green leaf. I went over to the leaf and nudged at it until the bug tumbled out, and then held it up on my fingertip.

"Ladybug, ladybug," I said under my breath, because Harvey was watching, *"fly away home."*

"Oh wow, Sabrina, I'm so sorry," said Harvey. "I've just remembered I have to go home."

I smiled and kissed him. "Is that so?"

Harvey cupped my face in his hands. "The woods are changed because you are made of ice and gold," he informed me seriously.

"Um, thanks. Thank you for that," I told him. "Goodbye, now."

That matter settled, I headed toward my destination, past the shadows of the woods to the clear line of the stream.

But I didn't make it to the clearing, or the creek. I had barely taken a few steps before I heard a familiar sound. Like falling leaves, except louder.

They dropped from the sky as if they were dropping out of the trees like three wicked, gleaming apples, but I knew better. Witches came from the sky, not the trees. Their three shadows fell over me, streaming long and dark.

Prudence, Agatha, and Dorcas. Agatha's black hair flew with the wind like a flag made of darkness, and Dorcas's red hair mingled with hers like a flag made of flame. They looked powerful and strange, picture-perfect witches, but it was Prudence who was the really dangerous one.

Prudence's hair was bleached nearly bone white to contrast with her flawless dark skin. Her lips curled into the sneer that was Prudence's default expression, or at least Prudence's default expression around me.

"The woods are changed because of I-can't-believe-what-I-just-heard and gold." Prudence tipped back her head and laughed. "Oh, Sabrina, Sabrina, what have you done?"

Agatha and Dorcas echoed Prudence's laughter, as they echoed most things about Prudence. Their black and red heads bent together, sisterly and close. They weren't really sisters, but they always called themselves that.

Even they could be sure of each other. And they were the worst people I knew.

"Oooh, Henry, call me the rose of the world again!" cackled Agatha.

"His name is not—"

"Nothing you do could be boring!" cackled Dorcas. "Except literally *everything* you mortal lovebirds do is boring."

Their fingers were all linked, like little girls skipping off to the playground together. They dressed in clothes with the same cut, short skirts and high lace collars, a uniform for witches. Or sisters.

Prudence unlinked her fingers and wandered over to a tree,

sliding her arm around the trunk and caressing the bark. For a moment she looked like the world's nastiest dryad. When she glanced over at me, her dark eyes were even sharper than usual.

"You know," she said thoughtfully. "I have a wide experience of teenage boys. And they really, normally, do not speak like that. I mean, they're primitive life-forms, they can barely grunt. It's hard to make out even simple phrases like *Nice bod* and *Let's go out for a milkshake sometime.* I think our little Sabrina may have cast a spell on him."

Dorcas said throatily: "And now he's hers."

I tried to brush past them, but the three girls joined fingers again and blocked my way.

"Oh, no judgment, Sabrina! The path to hell is paved with broken men," said Prudence. "So, fun journey, fun destination, really. Except I thought mortals were so precious to you. Almost like real people, right?"

"You always act so high and mighty about us *ensorceling mortal boys and leading them to their doom*," Agatha said in a singsong voice. "But in the end, you're just like us."

Dorcas tossed her long hair over her shoulder like a red whip. "She *wishes* she could be like us."

Prudence strolled toward me, long legs eating the space between us in two strides, leaned down to get in my face, then jabbed at my shoulder with a long, glossy black fingernail until I fell back a step.

Softly, Prudence said: "But she never will."

When the Weird Sisters first sought me out in the woods, a few years ago, I was so excited. I didn't know any witches besides my aunts and my cousin, not really. It seemed ideal to meet three girls, the same number as my three mortal friends at school, as if I could mirror my experience of mortal life with them. I wanted them to be my friends, to tell me everything about magic and exactly what it was like at the Academy of Unseen Arts. It's hilarious to imagine now, but I wanted to love them.

Except they hated me. They sought me out so they could torment me, always declaring that a half witch was never going to be good enough. They don't want me at the Academy of Unseen Arts, and I don't know if I want to go to school with people like them.

I stopped falling back and glared at Prudence. "I'm nothing like you. And I'm not going to doom anybody."

"So why'd you do it, then, if not to break his mind and his heart and bend him to your will?" Prudence seemed genuinely puzzled. "Your behavior is senseless."

I usually don't let myself show weakness in front of the Weird Sisters, but this time I made a crucial mistake. I broke our gaze, dropping my eyes to the forest floor, and Prudence's laugh rippled among the leaves.

"You used a love spell on a mortal because you want him to *weally, weally wuv you*? Maybe even commit to you? What's he going to do, give you a promise ring when you skip off to the Academy of Unseen Arts?" Prudence laughed. "That's pathetic."

"It wasn't a *love spell*—"

"Are we feeling a little insecure about our dark baptism, half witch? Wondering if you can take your place among the witches and leave the mortals behind? Tell me all about your problems," said Prudence. "I love stories that make me laugh."

The words fell from her sneering mouth, bitter as poisoned apples. They were all the more bitter because they were true.

"Stay in the mortal world if you love it so much," said Dorcas venomously. "It would be better if you did. Everybody knows you're not cut out to be a witch."

"Yes, Sabrina," trilled Agatha. "I really think going through your dark baptism and coming to our school would be a mistake."

"You're the ones making a mistake," I said. "You're in my way."

I barreled through the barrier of their bodies, breaking apart Dorcas's and Agatha's joined hands. They were clearly the weak link, and I was past them and crashing through the trees before they could hurl a single spell at me.

"Can't bear to be apart from a mortal boy," Prudence called after me, as if she was a judge pronouncing a sentence. "Watch out, Sabrina. If you're too desperate for love *and* magic, you'll fall between two stools and get nothing. You'll be lost."

I had no answer for her. I ran away through the woods.

I didn't know why Prudence was always needling me. I didn't know why she had to be the way she was. I didn't know why she had always hated me so much.

WHAT HAPPENS IN THE DARK

Witches dream as mortals do.

Prudence, Agatha, and Dorcas have known each other since they were little. They didn't go to the Academy after their dark baptisms. They have always been there, three tiny girls walking hand in hand in hand through the halls, living with the towering statue, between the stone walls of the edifice that looked more crypt than school. The harshness of the Academy shaped the Weird Sisters, and they don't expect life to be anything but hard.

It's Sabrina's own fault, and her own foolishness, that she does. It's not Prudence's problem. Prudence has her own problems to deal with.

Witches' lives are dangerous, and orphans are not uncommon. Their High Priest took them in and is caring for them.

They're lucky, Father Blackwood tells them: especially as witches aren't exactly rare. Not like warlocks. Boys might find homes, but orphan girls never will.

They call themselves the Weird Sisters, and when everyone else starts calling them that too, it feels like a triumph. Everyone told Prudence she had no family, but now, through her own will, she has sisters.

And sisters share.

"I can't exactly give all three of you my letter ring, or class jacket, or whatever the mortals call it," the Weird Sisters' warlock boyfriend, Nick Scratch, told Prudence in the woods on Sunday—the day for restless sin—and Prudence realized to her insulted astonishment that he was breaking up with her.

With all of them, through her, which is pure laziness.

When she tells him so, Nick flashes the bright, insincerely charming smile that first attracted them.

"Idle hands do the devil's work," he said. "So I have to keep super idle, in the service of the Dark Lord."

Prudence rolled her eyes. It's amazing how much effort men will put in so they don't have to make an effort. Dorcas and Agatha will be disappointed, though. They really liked Nick. He made a change from tormenting mortal boys. But then, Prudence thinks, who needs a change from tormenting mortal boys? It's the best.

She shrugged. "Of course none of us want you to do ridiculous mortal things with jackets and rings. Why would you bring that up?"

Nick shrugged too. That was one of the best things about him, Prudence had always thought. He was one of the few witches she'd met who could pretend to be magnificently indifferent as well as she did. Sometimes when they were together, the sheer force of both their façades made them seem almost real.

Maybe she liked Nick a little too.

"Is this about us creating all those super sexy illusions?" Prudence bit out. "Was it too sexy for you to handle?"

"Nothing's too sexy for me to handle. Still, it's not my favorite thing you do," Nick admitted. "Things can be real as well as magical. But it's not entirely that."

"Then what?"

"I don't know," said Nick, his voice soft, and if he was going to be soft Prudence had no use for him. "Don't you ever feel like there must be something more?"

"More than eternal beauty, awesome power, and a life well spent in the hellfire-warm bosom of Satan?" Prudence sneered. "I really don't."

Whatever Nick meant, it's clear he doesn't think he could find this something more in *her*.

"Did you meet someone?" demanded Prudence. "Did you meet *someones?*"

Nick smiled in a way she was not familiar with and did not like. Seeing Nick Scratch dreamy-eyed made Prudence feel unwell. "Almost."

"What do you mean?"

"Maybe I'm waiting," said Nick, "for the key to every secret in the universe."

Prudence scoffed. They were all broken up, then. She'll tell her sisters later, and cheer them up the only way she knows how: by hurting someone else.

Maybe she can go find that half witch.

Sabrina annoys the ever-loving Satan out of Prudence. Everyone at the Academy talks about her: the half-mortal daughter of the former and late High Priest. If Edward Spellman had married one of his own kind, his child could have been High Priest after him. As it is, she's a joke. People shake their heads pityingly about her, more than they ever did about Prudence and her sisters. It's nice to have someone lower on the social scale, but unlike the stupid, happily oblivious mortals, aware enough to understand how low she is. The Weird Sisters can always find time in their day to make how inferior she is clear to Sabrina.

The first time Prudence ever saw Sabrina, Sabrina was walking hand in hand with her aunt Hilda. The coven whispered about Hilda Spellman: too soft, everybody agreed, and her commitment to the Dark Lord was doubtful at best. She'd gone too easy on that cousin she'd raised, and that was how he went wrong. Hilda had eyes blue as heaven: simply horrible.

No doubt the woman would be too soft with the half-mortal girl too. They looked too soft, Sabrina in a yellow raincoat and a knitted scarf, kicking up red and gold leaves. Her aunt was fussing over Sabrina, adjusting her scarf. Prudence leaned her cold cheek against the cold bark of a tree and closed her eyes so she wouldn't have to see any more.

After Nick broke up with them, Prudence searched for Sabrina, but she didn't find her until Sabrina was already walking around the curve of the road onto Spellman ground, past the sign for the Spellman mortuary and the tree that spread its branches over the small cluster of graves out front.

Prudence wasn't scared of anything, but she wasn't fool enough to cross Zelda Spellman on her own turf. Nobody talked about Zelda being too soft.

Prudence would come back for Sabrina another time, with her sisters. She was about to turn away when she saw a curtain twitch, in a small window in an upper story of that house of slanting roofs and many windows. A boy was in the window, looking out for Sabrina's coming.

Prudence eats boys for a snack and has room for apples of knowledge after, but this one's a five-course meal with chocolate cake for dessert. *Well done, Sabrina,* Prudence thought for a startled moment, and wondered what Sabrina was doing messing around with some pathetic human boy when she had all this at home. Then Prudence realized this must be the wayward cousin.

When the cousin saw Sabrina, his face changed. He'd looked a little sad before.

It made Prudence wonder suddenly how it would be to have someone waiting for you. To get a smile like that, wide as an ocean and bright as the sun, just for walking up the lane.

Sabrina must be used to it.

Prudence advanced through the trees, wandering closer to get a better look.

The cousin swung the door casually open for Sabrina as she climbed the front steps, though he must have moved fast to get from the window to the door in that time. He slung Sabrina's stupid schoolbag on his shoulder, and she tugged at the little velvet scarf around his neck, and the door of the Spellman house closed behind them.

The kitchen was around the back, a cozy room with skull-patterned wallpaper and hanging herbs. Prudence could see teal-painted cupboards as she moved nearer, walking softly through the twigs and leaves scattered over the ground. The aunt with the silly fond eyes was attending to something

bubbling on the black iron stove, and beamed as if with startled joy when the cousin and Sabrina whirled in. It made
Prudence want to scream. The cousin was literally enchanted
not to leave the house. Sabrina had lived there all her life. It
couldn't possibly be a surprise to see them.

Sabrina snapped her fingers, and faint music started to
play. She and the cousin wove around the kitchen chairs, half
dancing and half play-fighting, ducking under the bundles of
dried herbs, as the aunt threw up her hands in mock dismay
and laughed at their antics.

"Don't you know I'm only human?" Sabrina sang, like it was a
joke between them, instead of a hideous truth she should be
ashamed of.

Sabrina still had hold of the cousin's scarf, and the cousin
ducked his head so she could loop the velvet around his neck
again, leading him on a leash and dancing backward while he
sang the next line of the song to her. Something about being
there for her, while Sabrina wagged a finger at him, mischievous and young in a way Prudence had never been. Then the
cousin seized hold of the aunt's waist, and the three of them
were suddenly dancing in a ridiculous conga line around the
kitchen table.

Something more, said Nick's voice in her mind, yearning, as if
he'd instinctively felt a lack she hadn't. Not until she saw what
she was missing.

Prudence turned away, abruptly sick of them all, and stormed off through the woods.

Prudence had been forged by fire and hammered by countless blows into something harder than stone, the dark jewel in the bone crown of the coven of the Church of Night. There was nothing Sabrina Spellman had that Prudence envied.

She returned to the Academy and sang in the Infernal Choir. She has always been the best singer, and every time she thinks Lady Blackwood will be impressed with her. Her High Priest's wife will see Prudence has amazing potential, and she'll invite Prudence to a special private dinner with her and Father Blackwood. Except that never happens. Every time, Lady Blackwood glares at Prudence, and seems to hate Prudence more.

Prudence spends hours plotting ways to get her heart's desire. She wants to sit on a throne of skulls, revered by her entire coven, dark and glorious as midnight. She wants what any witch would want, but she wants it harder.

Sometimes, going to sleep between the cold walls of the Academy, in the circle of dormitory beds, Prudence allows herself to admit certain things that she could not with a waking mind.

If she had only one wish, she thinks at those times, it would be for Father Blackwood to be her real father, and the Weird Sisters her real sisters.

That night, Prudence lets herself dream of how it would be to have what Sabrina has, even just for one day.

She would run up the steps of the Spellman house, and that beautiful boy would be waiting to open the door for her, with such a smile. That sweet-faced woman would be cooking in the kitchen, making all the food she liked best. When it was night, she'd curl up under the soft blankets in that fancy wrought-iron bed in her very own room, and she'd be warm.

She'd be home.

OH, LOOK IN THE MIRROR

The trees seemed to open up as I ran to the clearing, branches and thorns bending backward for me, green grass beneath my feet like a carpet being rolled out to welcome me.

I crashed through the trees into the clearing, and the silence.

The spirit of the wishing well was lying on the riverbank, her skirts spread out on the grass. The grass did not even bend under her body. Her skirt seemed to be made of the same stuff as her skin, some magic liquid only a touch more solid and opaque than water that glistened like tears.

I pulled up short and said blankly: "You're not in your well."

"I was waiting for you," the spirit of the wishing well told me in her shivery, silvery voice. "I was hoping you would come."

She gave me a shimmering beckon, and I felt the same urge as in the Hall of Mirrors. I went to sit by her side. Her smile was moon-bright, if the moon had chosen to shine only on me.

"I am so glad you are here," said the spirit. "But you look sad. Why is that?"

I hesitated. She reached out and took my hand in hers. Her skin was cool, but so was moonlight, and that was made for witches.

Her voice flowed over me like a river over a stone on the riverbed, moved by its currents. "Tell me."

Then I poured it all out: the spell Ambrose and I had done, the doubts I had, the way I wanted to be a witch but keep hold of the mortal life I cherished, the way my aunts always spoke as if that would not be possible, the way the Weird Sisters said that I didn't have what it took to be one of them. Harvey, and my parents: that my parents had found a way, and I wanted to be like them, and I couldn't see how.

When all my secrets were poured out, I lifted my gaze to her face. I'd read the phrase *her eyes were pools* before, but this woman's eyes were literally pools: crystal lakes, with the image of my own pain caught in them.

"Oh, my dear," whispered the spirit of the well. "I am so sorry. From the first moment I saw you, I knew that you had great potential for power, but now I see you have a great heart too. Of course they don't understand you."

"Who?" I said.

"Those unworthy witch girls," hissed the spirit, her voice like a dammed river breaking its bounds, angry enough to be almost menacing. "Your mortal friends, your family, this cousin Ambrose of yours with his cold, fickle heart. Especially Ambrose. If that spell goes wrong, it was your cousin's spell, not yours. His fault, not yours. None of them can understand you, because none of them feel as you do."

"Being half witch and half mortal," I whispered.

"It's more than that," said the spirit of the wishing well. "You're more than that. You're made of finer stuff than they are. You're special. You're better in every way."

I remembered how she had spoken of me wearing a crown. As if she had seen me, somehow different than I was now, seen the me I wanted people to see.

I licked my dry lips. "What did you mean," I asked, "when you said I was born to be a witch of legend?"

The spirit smiled a gleaming smile, and murmured one word.

"Look."

She gestured to the stream she was lying beside, and droplets fell from her fingertips as though she could summon a tiny shower of rain. The droplets rained into the clear waters and turned them silver, stopped the rushing course of the river and turned it smooth. I leaned over and found the river had become my looking glass.

Only, as in the Hall of Mirrors, somehow my reflection was transformed.

In the glassy waters was a girl beautiful as the dawn, but somehow I knew she was me. That girl was tall as I would never be, with the glamour of my aunt Zelda and the sweet softness of my aunt Hilda and the fairy-tale-princess beauty of my mother's photograph. That girl walked with her head held magnificently high through the halls of Baxter High School, her hands alive with pale fire. Everybody knew she was a witch, and they only admired her more for it. She was so strong that nobody ever dared touch her friends.

I stirred and asked: "How—?"

There were ripples in the pool, as if in answer: Suddenly a whole world blossomed around the beauty who was me. I could see my friends by her side suddenly, Roz with her eyes clear and brilliant with admiration, Susie striding in perfect confidence that she was safe with me. And Harvey, holding my hand, his lips moving as we walked, making the same shape over and over again. I couldn't hear him, but I knew

Harvey was saying *I love you*, and it was real, and it was right, and it was perfect.

"Do you see?" asked the water spirit eagerly. "Do you see what you could be?"

"I see..." I said, faltering.

"Shall I show you more?"

The waters rippled again, and the surroundings of the magical beauty changed. I saw myself walking home on the path through the trees, and the Weird Sisters came flying toward me, Prudence first, all their faces lit up with welcome for their sister. And then we did magic together out in the woods, and they were amazed at the magic I could do. I could turn the sun to the moon at noonday.

"Don't you want to be as beautiful as the morning?" asked the spirit.

"Yes," I whispered. "But—"

"Don't you want to be a queen among witches?"

"Yes," I whispered. "But—"

"Be brave enough to want," said the spirit. "If you are brave enough, you could have your heart's desire."

That towering, magical, gloriously powerful beauty turned her radiantly white-gold head back to the path as if she heard a call. She sprang up and ran back to the path through the woods. She was fast as if she flew, and nobody in the world could catch her, unless she wanted to be caught. On the curving road stood my cousin, not just in jeans and a shirt but in a jacket and boots. He was free but coming home, because his home was with me. I'd never cared that much about beauty, but this, getting to be both magical and beloved, was all I wanted. Ambrose pulled me into a tight hug, and I knew what he was saying too: *I love you, cousin.* We walked together and I knew what waited for us around the familiar curve in the road. My home, with my aunts, but not only my aunts. My mother and father waited for me there, as eager to see me as I was to see them. They all loved me, I was so beloved, because I was lovely, because I was all things lovable, and that meant I could keep everything I loved.

The girl in the mirror was all the things I could never be, and had all the things I could never have, yet somehow she was *me*.

"This is how I see you, and I see the truth of what you could be. You could have all this," murmured the spirit. "If you did the spell with my waters."

A spell you can only do with the waters of the wishing well, to unlock your true potential. Only certain witches can do it. The ones with the potential to be great.

I pulled away from her a fraction, letting her cool hand slip from mine. "Why are you telling me all this?"

"It's not that I chose you," said the spirit. "Destiny chose you. I am only a servant of Fate. And you. I am only a humble spirit, but I long to be part of greater things, and do great deeds. Those witch girls who hate you would kill for the power I am offering you, would spill oceans of blood for a drop of my magical waters, but I would never allow it. They could never be worthy. Only you are."

She lifted the hand I had dropped to touch my hair. I saw the lock of my hair held in that shining hand: My hair was an ordinary blond, but captured between her fingers the lock was lent the luster of her skin. I remembered the ice-and-gold hair of the girl who was me made beautiful as the morning.

The spirit smiled a shimmering smile. "I think you must be unique, Sabrina Spellman. I have never let another witch use the waters from my well or stream, but I would let you. It would be my honor to be part of your legend."

"Well," I said.

"Wish," she encouraged me. "Only wish for what you want, and your wish will come true. Plunge your hand to the wrist in my waters, and say the words, and have your heart's desire."

I reached out, and plunged my hand into the water past the wrist. The river was cool as her hand had been, cool as moonlight shining on another clearing in these woods, where I had been born and where I belonged.

"Mirror, mirror," whispered the spirit, like a plea, like a prayer. *"Make me fairer. Face and heart."*

"Mirror, mirror," I whispered back. *"Make me fairer. Face and heart."*

Who didn't want to be better, inside and out? Face and heart, and the world. The whole world should be more fair, should stop threatening to tear me away from one thing or the other that I loved. If I had the power, I could change everything.

It was as if I could feel everything changing already. There was a shimmer in my vision, and a sweet taste at the back of my throat as if I'd just drunk something delicious. I could feel the tiny hairs on my arm prickle and be soothed by the flow of water enveloping my skin.

Then a human voice broke through the sound of trees and wind, the last cool breath of dying summer. Sharp when everything had been going so smoothly, the voice called out: *"Sabrina!"*

WHAT HAPPENS IN THE DARK

Mary Wardwell longs to believe in magic.

      She always loved stories, and for a time she wanted to be a librarian, but the idea of being a teacher ended up appealing to her more. There is so much potential in children. Having so many eyes on her when she teaches class makes her nervous, but she enjoys watching their faces light up when they learn. Children look like the beginning of a story.

    She was young and brimful of promise herself, once. She was the only child of elderly parents, growing up bookish and excruciatingly shy, especially with children her own age. She didn't have many friends, but she took long walks in the woods and told herself everything would be different when she grew up. Once she'd finished her time in school, she kissed her parents goodbye and went off for adventures in the big city.

Her most vivid memory of the city is being on a train rattling through the night toward her tiny studio apartment. She remembers herself on that train as a young girl sitting at the edge of a threadbare green seat, so frayed there were brown holes and patches in it. The train had stopped in a tunnel for more than an hour, and through sheer pressure of boredom the passengers inside dropped the pretense they were not sharing transport and started talking to one another. There was a boy and a girl sitting across from her, about Mary's age or a little older, with colors in their hair and piercings, darkly lined eyes regarding her with mingled sympathy and scorn. When the train finally moved, they said they were on their way to a party, and invited her to join them. The mere idea was so glittering, so exciting, that it was too frightening. Mary said no. She said maybe another time.

But another time never came. She never saw those glamorous strangers again. She never went to any parties.

She did not even last a year in the city.

Her parents got sick, and she went home to care for them. By the time her parents died, she found she didn't have the courage to go back. Mary was terrified of exchanging trees for towers.

So she became a teacher in Greendale, and she chose to live in the littlest, loneliest house. Love for her did come, but it came late. Since faraway love and a little house were not altogether enough for a story-hungry soul, she began to collect the stories of the town. Memories were tucked away in books like pressed flowers, so their color and scent would last, waiting for her to discover them. Greendale was where she had been born and where she had chosen to belong. Those stories were her stories too, and if she did not learn them, the stories might be forgotten.

Mary read somewhere once that memories were the bones of the soul. So, in a way, she believes that piecing together the history of the town means keeping the foundations of Greendale firm. Some of the stories are too incredible to believe, but Mary Wardwell tries to believe them. Someone has to.

The oldest stories of the town are only shreds, no longer adding up to entire tales, but Mary finds them fascinating. There are lovely superstitions about secrets lurking in the mines, witches dancing in the woods. There are two brief accounts of a brave girl called Freya who fed her family when they were bound in the ice. There are descriptions of fierce hunters who saved the town. Times must have been hard back then.

Mary Wardwell laughed when she read an ancient scribble in an old book that read *Never go into the woods after dark*. She wept over the stories of witches, astonishingly hanged in her town as well as Salem. She told Susie Putnam once that she should be very proud of a heroic ancestor, and Susie was clearly puzzled, but just as clearly pleased.

Mary Wardwell likes to think of herself as the one who tells the town the story of itself. The past passes on candles to the future if you put out your hands to take the light.

She's the record keeper, the keeper of faith. She has the fanciful notion that as long as she keeps the books and lives in this little house in the midst of the wild woods, nothing truly bad can ever happen in her town.

THE SMALL HOUSE IN THE DARK WOODS

I stared in disbelief as my teacher appeared from between the clusters of trees. This was a clearing of silvery shadows, of moonlit magic. Someone wearing a tweed suit and spectacles seemed utterly out of place.

"My dear Sabrina! If you don't watch out, you could fall into the river. Then you would have a long walk home soaked to the skin. You might catch a chill."

I shuffled guiltily away from the river's edge.

"Uh, Ms. Wardwell. Hi. What are you doing here?"

Ms. Wardwell blinked at me behind her giant spectacles. "I live close by, and I was gathering flowers in the woods. I have an extensive dried flower collection."

"Oh," I said, and let the irony of my fib to Harvey sink in. "I didn't know people actually did that anymore."

I'd forgotten that Ms. Wardwell lived in that lonely house far from town, the only house in the woods. How strange it must be for a mortal to live there. I wondered if Ms. Wardwell ever heard the screams of witches celebrating. She probably imagined they were foxes.

"You're far from home, Sabrina," Ms. Wardwell remarked. "Are you hiking by yourself? It's almost dark. Remember, it's not summer anymore."

"Just... on a nature walk," I answered.

Ms. Wardwell hesitated. "Would you like to come to my house for a cup of tea, since you are so close by? You can warm up by the fire before you go home."

Ms. Wardwell looked so timid, and so hopeful. It would have been cruel to refuse her. Even though all I wanted was to return to the spirit, and my spell.

"Oh, sure," I told her. "Thanks very much."

I followed Ms. Wardwell, but before I left I whispered a promise to the wind and the spirit I knew was listening beneath the water:

"I'll come back."

✳✳✳

Ms. Wardwell lived in a tiny cottage near the very edge of the deep woods. Her home made me think of the gingerbread cottage in fairy tales where a witch might live. Except instead of a witch luring guests into her cottage, a strange witch was being invited into this one.

There was a horseshoe hammered over the door: a piece of cold iron, meant to keep away fairies. When I stepped inside, I saw things like that everywhere.

The whole place was terribly quaint. There was a clock shaped like a teapot on the wall. There was a crucifix over the hearth fire with a painting behind it. Aunt Zelda always pointedly averted her eyes when presented with what she called *images of the false god.*

I stirred the tea in my teacup with my tiny silver spoon and said awkwardly: "Love what you've done with the place. Thanks for having me."

"Thank you for coming," said Ms. Wardwell. "I don't have many visitors. Though I have found several young people rambling by that river near dark, and I do ask them in for a cup of tea. I can't think why that spot draws them so."

"I suppose they're wishing in the wishing well."

"Is that well a wishing well?" Ms. Wardwell asked with interest. "I've never heard that before. I must make a note of that. I collect town legends, you know. I consider myself the unofficial town historian."

"Oh, right." I scratched my head, dislodging my hairband slightly, and smiled. Ms. Wardwell and her cottage both seemed a little silly to me, but sweet.

"Oh, yes," said Ms. Wardwell. "Not many people realize

that we have a long history of witches in Greendale, to rival the stories of Salem."

I took a careful sip of hot tea. "That is absolutely news to me. How interesting. And new. To me. Something I have never heard before in all my life. Ever."

Ms. Wardwell glowed at the expression of interest. She jumped up from her wingback chair, spilling some tea as she did so, to take a large, leather-bound book down from a high shelf.

"Would you like to hear this contemporary account of a witch?" she asked. "It's said to have been written by an ancestor of the Putnams."

"The Putnams, as in my friend Susie Putnam?" I asked, lost. "Yes, of course."

"The young witch came to me again yesterday," Ms. Wardwell read aloud. *"She speaks in riddles, but sweetly. She says she will be kind for my kindness to her kind. The crops this year looked to fail, but now we think the crops are flourishing late. Perhaps it is only chance, but everywhere the crops are growing now are places the young witch walked yesterday. I can see her now, Freya of the long hair and the summer song, with the edge of her gown lost in the green grass. Surely God made her. The devil could not make anything so lovely."*

Ms. Wardwell replaced the book on the shelf and began to talk about the fact that some believed the account was written by an eccentric, or somebody writing a short story, and nobody was sure which one of the Putnams it was, whether it was a man or a woman, and others said it was not one of the Putnams who wrote the account at all.

Ms. Wardwell didn't know the account was real, but I did.

Imagine one of the mortals knowing someone was a witch, suspecting they were doing magic before their very eyes, and still writing about them with such affection. Imagine mortals and witches, able to live in peace.

I'm sure that was how my mother thought about my father. I'm sure she loved his magic and understood him. If I told Harvey the truth, was that how he would feel about me? I wished I knew.

Witch-hunters had come for the witches of Greendale. My aunts always said I could never tell a mortal the truth, and I never had. But I wanted to.

"Forgive me, Sabrina," said Ms. Wardwell, taking her seat again. "I get carried away when I talk about my hobbies. What is it you were wishing for, when you went to the wishing well? You always seem so happy at school. I would have imagined you have nothing to wish for."

I thought of the visions the spirit of the wishing well had showed me. I imagined being a great witch, so powerful I could make the moon shine at noonday, having all the love and magic I desired.

I said slowly: "I have a lot to wish for. There's a boy…"

"Harvey Kinkle," Ms. Wardwell supplied. "Sweet boy. Shouldn't draw so many pictures in class, of course."

"Harvey," I said. "And my friends. And my family. I wish I knew how they would feel, if they knew everything there was to know about me. I have a big decision to make soon, and my family are expecting me to make them proud, but they don't know how many doubts I have about it. I haven't told them. And I keep so many secrets from Harvey and my friends, and that can't be right, but it would be wrong to tell them. I keep thinking about what I should do, because I'm really not sure what to do. I'm not sure of anything. And I'm always sure."

It wasn't like talking to the spirit of the wishing well. I had been able to tell her everything. She'd been able to understand everything, and still see me as someone great. That had been everything I wanted.

Ms. Wardwell couldn't even see me for what I was. She was a sweet, silly woman who thought witches were stories and owned a teapot clock. I didn't understand why I was even trying.

But Ms. Wardwell surprised me by slipping off her chair, taking my hands in hers, and kneeling at my feet. Her face was not smooth and perfect as that of the wishing-well spirit, and it was not opaque either. I was startled by the depths of sympathy and sweetness in her green eyes. I realized Ms.

Wardwell was actually very beautiful. Perhaps Ms. Wardwell didn't know that herself.

"I'm sorry, Sabrina," she murmured. "Of course it must feel terrible to find yourself floundering in uncertainty. Especially if this is the first time you have been truly unsure."

I nodded, fighting back tears.

"But my dear, what a wonderful gift you have," said Ms. Wardwell. "To be almost always certain. Most people aren't sure about anything. Though, if I had that power, if I could be that sure of myself, I would feel as though I had a key to enchantment."

The fire in the hearth was warm and comforting, and so was the clasp of my teacher's hands. With darkness gathering behind the windows, the little cottage didn't seem absurd to me any longer. It was cozy and inviting, a small, glowing refuge from the darkest depths of the woods. Even a witch could feel welcome here.

"I'm not a very wise woman," Ms. Wardwell confessed. "There's no particular reason you should listen to me. But if I were to give one piece of advice, it would be: Don't fear that you are not enough. That's the only fear that can stop you." She hesitated. "Does that sound silly?"

"No," I murmured. "No, it doesn't sound silly at all, Ms. Wardwell. Thank you very much."

***

I walked home through the full dark of the woods by night. Ms. Wardwell tried to insist on accompanying me, but I said I knew the way.

I didn't tell her I'd been born in these woods. No mortal knew these woods as I did.

But I carried Ms. Wardwell's kind words with me as I went. On my way, I paused at the place I would have to turn, to go back to the stream and the clearing and the well.

I decided not to go. Not tonight.

Instead I chose a different path, and cut through the deepest part of the woods to a valley glowing with moonlight, as if the valley were a green cup full of silver liquid. I dimly remembered my aunt Hilda telling me tales of goblins living there.

I sighed and said: "I swear I would do the right thing. If only I knew what it was."

If the goblins heard me, they didn't answer.

I went home, the slanted rooftops of my house barely visible against the sky, but every window burning yellow. I hurried inside and heard my aunt Zelda's voice ringing from above, and ran up the split-level stairs to find my aunts and Ambrose in the hallway outside my bedroom. Aunt Hilda was hanging back. Ambrose was stretched out on the floor. Aunt Zelda was holding a bucket, for some reason, and applying the pointed toe of her high-heeled shoe to Ambrose's ribs.

"Would you stop it, Ambrose! You play the fool so much sometimes I worry that you are not playing."

"Don't worry, Auntie Z.," Ambrose answered. "I'm always playing."

I said, breathless from my race up the stairs: "Hey, guys, what's going on?"

"Ah, Sabrina," said Aunt Zelda. "Thank hell you are home. Your little mortal boyfriend has been causing trouble."

I was instantly struck with alarm.

"Harvey was here?" I demanded. "When I wasn't here? What happened to him? What did you do?"

"It isn't what we did," Aunt Zelda snapped. "It's what that ridiculous mortal did. He stood under your bedroom window and attempted to serenade you."

My mouth fell open. "He didn't."

My shy Harvey would never do that.

"I am sorry to say that he did," declared Aunt Zelda. "Your mortal suitor does not have a melodious voice. At first I believed the sound was cats fighting to the death, but that happy dream was dashed when I made out the words. Tell her, Ambrose."

Ambrose was lying full-length on the floor. He appeared to be actually crying with laughter.

"He sang a song," he confirmed. "I can sing it for you, if you like. I wouldn't want you to feel you'd missed out on anything, cousin. I can remember every glorious word. I will never forget. They are written on my heart in letters of fire. Shall I begin? *Oh, Sabrina, oh, Sabrina, as soon as I seen ya—*"

My hand flew to cover my open mouth.

"Be quiet, Ambrose," commanded Aunt Zelda.

"But I haven't even got to the bit where his love is like a yellow, yellow daffodil!"

"Hush, love," murmured Aunt Hilda. "That's not kind."

"Please just let me tell her about the part where he sang that she was the powdered sugar to his donut and if she was a trash can he'd be a fox!"

Aunt Zelda's tone was menacing. "I can fill this bucket again and dump it over you, and if I am forced to listen to that song again, I will."

"I thought it was very romantic, really," Aunt Hilda muttered. "His little face was so sad and surprised when you dumped the bucket out the window."

I realized what my aunts were saying.

"You *dumped* a bucket of *water* onto Harvey?" I snarled.

Aunt Zelda pursed her lips. "Was it water or pig's blood? Can you remember, Ambrose? Anyway, he went quiet after that."

I breathed: "Oh no. I have to call him."

"That's an excellent idea, Sabrina," said Aunt Zelda. "Tell him that if he ever sings on my property again, I will have owls consume his tongue."

Hilda made a face. "Maybe put it a bit more tactfully than that, love."

Aunt Zelda flounced off to her bedroom, her heels making angry clicking sounds on the parquet floor. Aunt Hilda hurried after her, making soothing noises. I stepped over Ambrose on my way to my room, but before I could slam my bedroom door, Ambrose rolled across the rug in a flurry of silk robe and continued laughter. He tossed a conspiratorial grin up to me, as if this was a joke, as if Harvey was a joke to him.

"Looks like our spell worked a little too well, cousin."

I remembered what the spirit of the wishing well had told me.

"It wasn't our spell," I said coldly. "It was your spell."

WHAT HAPPENS IN THE DARK

She knows the dark was created so that terrible things might happen to beautiful creatures.

She is not particularly disturbed by Sabrina's failure to return.

Humans have bursts of wild hope. At certain turns of the moon, they gain confidence in themselves, they believe in love or mercy, set their hearts on the beauty of the world they can see or the grace of another world they cannot, and tell themselves that is enough.

But hope, like humans themselves, does not last. Sooner or later, faith fades, and doubts creep in. She doesn't do anything to make it happen. She doesn't have to. They do it to themselves. They always come crawling back, begging for greatness, dying to be saved from the worst they fear themselves to be.

She knows how to be patient, and now she is playing a game for a bigger prize than any before. She has her orders. She knows what to do. She knows what humans are. Not a soul who walks the earth, witch or mortal, is truly sure of themselves. They just wish they were.

All she must do is lie by the river and wait.

HEARTS AND ROSES

I was eating breakfast with Ambrose and Aunt Hilda when the knock on the door came Tuesday. That meant, horrifyingly, that Aunt Zelda answered.

"I am fond of music," was her opening greeting. "But I cannot describe what I experienced last night as music."

I swallowed my mouthful of cereal and gave a pointed cough over the startled murmur of a boy's voice.

Even before last night's serenade, there were times when Aunt Zelda had been extremely rude to Harvey, but I'd spoken to her strongly about being a gracious hostess.

"I mean, ah yes, hello, Harvey," Aunt Zelda said with dignity. "Fine moon we had last night, wasn't it? I do get a thrill from a crescent moon. They look rather like daggers."

Unfortunately, this was Aunt Zelda's idea of being a gracious hostess.

I pushed back bowl and chair. "Gotta go."

"When shall we three meet again?" asked Ambrose, who seemed blissfully unaware that I was angry with him. "Oh, right, when you come home from school. Because I never leave the house, and Auntie H.'s most frequent trip is out to the graveyard. Auntie H. and I are ready for another exciting day crafting exquisite paper helicopters. Paper planes ceased to be a challenge fifty years ago."

Aunt Hilda waved her spatula admonishingly at him.

I ran for the door. Harvey hadn't answered his phone last night. He must be absolutely humiliated. The last thing he needed right now was Aunt Zelda. I had to save him.

Saving him was not the problem.

When I got to the door, I found a broad-shouldered miner's son on our porch. The wrong one.

"Aunt *Z*.!" I exclaimed. "That is *not Harvey*! That is his brother, Tommy!"

"I have been trying to tell her that," Tommy said mildly.

"Oh." Aunt Zelda frowned, then waved off the whole situation with her cigarette. "I did think he looked slightly different than he does usually."

I seized her by the elbow and dragged her away from Tommy and the door.

"Like, that he had a *different face?*" I hissed.

"Mortals all look the same to me," Aunt Zelda whispered back. "They both wear simply hideous flannel shirts. It's like they're trying to confuse me."

"I give up," I told her. "Let's go, Tommy."

I dashed outside, grabbed Tommy's flannel sleeve, and began dragging him down the porch steps. Tommy's face was baffled. I didn't blame him.

"Goodbye, Other Harvey," called Aunt Zelda.

I made an apologetic face at Tommy.

"She's a character, your aunt," Tommy remarked.

He didn't seem unduly bothered by the fact that my aunt couldn't recognize my own boyfriend. I guess the whole town expects us to be weird, but I couldn't help feeling ashamed. Aunt Zelda and Ambrose are always dismissive of Harvey. Aunt Hilda is kind to him, but Aunt Hilda is kind to everyone. Sometimes I wonder if she's kind to Harvey in the same way she would pet a dog.

"You could say that," I said. "Er, not that I'm not pleased to see you—hi, Tommy!—but I've seen more of you in the last few days than I have in years. Can I ask what you're doing here? Where's Harvey?"

Tommy opened the door of his red truck for me. "Harvey asked me to take you to school. He said he had a surprise waiting there for you. He said it was an apology for last night."

I scrambled into the truck, assailed by a fresh wave of guilt. "There's no need for him to apologize to me."

Tommy got in behind the wheel. "Sabrina, what happened last night? Harvey was gone for a while, and when he came back, his shirt was…"

"Was it pig's blood?" I asked, and then changed my mind. "Wait, maybe don't answer that. Maybe I don't want to know."

Tommy's eyebrows were practically in orbit. "Does this have anything to do with your aunt talking about music?" he guessed.

"Maybe I don't want to talk about it at all."

Tommy nodded obligingly, and drove on through the woods. Some of the leaves on the trees were turning gold. It felt like only yesterday the trees had been all summer green.

"Harvey's been really weird lately," Tommy offered at last, his voice soft. "I think it's my fault."

I twisted my hands together in my lap. "It's not your fault, Tommy. It's mine."

"Oh," said Tommy. "Did you guys have a fight?"

I didn't answer. I didn't know how to explain. We drove in awkward, terrible silence until we drew near Baxter High, and Tommy drew in a deep, incredulous breath.

"Oh, no, no," he murmured. The truck slammed to a halt, and Tommy grasped my elbow. I stared up at him, alarmed by the sudden urgency in Tommy's usually easy drawl. "Sabrina, *please* don't break up with him. He's gone too far and I'll tell him so, but you're his world. Please don't break my little brother's heart."

"I would never break up with Harvey," I answered, bewildered.

Tommy gave me a brief, strained smile. "I'll hold you to that."

He leaped from the truck, and I leaned forward in my seat, peering through the windshield. For a moment I only saw the familiar redbrick and crenellated rooftops, the middle roof flat and the other two coming to sharp peaks, of Baxter High.

Then my eyes fell on the black iron railing around the school, and I saw what Tommy had seen. It felt as if the brightness blurred my vision for a moment, as if I was staring into the sun, but I was only looking into the hearts of flowers.

The morning sky was hazy blue, the brightest blue of summer barely lost. The black fence surrounding the school was usually like a line drawn, cutting sharply across red building and blue sky. Today there were bright splashes of color twined through every wire link, splashes of crimson and yellow and lavender and green. Soft petals fell on the ground where groups of students walked, and to get to school they had to pass under an arch of starry color. The links of the fence had become silk ropes woven with a dozen different floral colors, and the steel frame of the fence was clustered with flowers so thick and bright they seemed like a woman's necklace shimmering with rubies and sapphires and garnets.

There were flowers of all kinds, but mostly roses. They looked like enchanted roses, which I'd read were always tempting to touch with hidden thorns. Their long stems were knotted around the wire of the fence or poked through the gates. Witches' roses decorating the outside of our school. The whole fence, almost the whole school, had been turned into a flowery wreath. Just for me.

Harvey was standing beside the brightest point in all his bright handiwork, his face vivid and expectant as the flowers. Roz and Susie were standing beside him. They didn't just look skeptical or stunned. They looked upset.

I fumbled the door handle three times, then managed to get out of the truck. By that time Tommy had already dashed up to the others and was talking to Roz and Susie while cupping Harvey's elbow. Then he headed straight for the principal—who was not going to take this well; Principal Hawthorne did not strike me as a fan of romantic gestures on school property—while calling out for the nurse.

I frowned. For the nurse?

There was brightness on the ground as well as suspended in the air. Red splashes were blooming on the earth at Harvey's feet. My mind lied to my eyes for a moment and told me they were flowers, only more flowers.

I ran to Harvey's side. His eyes, downcast by Tommy's approach, shone brilliant when he saw me.

"Sabrina! Do you like it? I made it for you."

I could not choke out my thanks past my horror. Instead, all I could do was tug on Harvey's sleeve and bring him stumbling along with me and away from everyone else.

Once we were a little distance apart from the growing crowd, I let go of his sleeve. With carefulness that came too late, with terrified gentleness, I used the very tips of my fingers to turn Harvey's artist's hands palms up.

His skin was scored with the cruel marks of thorns, palms slashed open. Even as I stared, fresh bright blood, red as roses, welled up in those ragged wounds.

I threw my book bag down on the ground and rummaged through its contents, emerging with the pouch of dried herbs Aunt Hilda made sure I always carried.

"Give me your hands, Harvey," I commanded, and he laid his poor, wounded hands in mine as trustfully as a child.

Close up, I could see the places where the thorns had bitten too deep. If he was left to himself, it would be weeks before Harvey could draw without wincing. He'd done this to make me happy, and not cared if he lost what made him happy. I hadn't been thinking selflessly of him, I'd selfishly wanted him to reassure me, and now he was hurt. I dropped a kiss and a tear onto his curled fingers, overwhelmed by how guilty I felt, and how sorry I was.

There was a note of genuine horror in Harvey's voice. "Sabrina, are you crying?"

"No, of course not." I whisked another tear from my eye, dabbed the herbs carefully on the cuts with a fingertip, and tried to concentrate. *"Rue and valerian, mint and basil. Cure all and save all, save every person born."*

Harvey blinked down into my eyes. "What's this?"

"It's a—poultice," I told him. "Some herbs. An herbal remedy. To stop your cuts from stinging."

"They hardly sting now," said Harvey. "Sabrina, I'm sorry I scared you, but look. I'm not hurt at all."

His face was frighteningly vulnerable, eager to please and not sure how he'd failed. He was so easy to hurt, and I'd never meant to, but I had hurt him. I fought down dread and wrenched my eyes from his face to his hands.

The magic had worked. I'd fixed him. Where there had been a crimson hatch of cuts was now just normal crisscrossing lines across his palms, beneath the tacky, fast-drying trail of blood mingled with herbs. No harm done.

The stomp of Tommy's boots echoed over Harvey's shoulder. Because I was holding Harvey's hands, I felt Harvey flinch, and I tensed, stricken with a sudden impulse to push Harvey behind me and fight anything that dared threaten him.

But then Tommy put his hands on Harvey's shoulders, grip obviously light. When Harvey glanced around, he saw his brother's face, and all the tension went out of him. Whatever it was Harvey feared, it wasn't his brother.

"Let me see your hands," said Tommy. Harvey displayed his hands, palm up as if to prove his innocence, and Tommy sighed with relief. "I thought—I only saw them for a moment, but I thought you'd actually hurt yourself. Where did you even find all these flowers?"

"The flowers were growing in the woods."

"Oh, sure," said Tommy. "There was a ton of gorgeous roses growing in the woods. I guess someone planted a giant romantic woodland garden. You're in trouble, and you're an idiot."

Neither of them knew there was dangerous magic in the woods, that some witch must have grown these roses and then forgotten them. Neither of them knew witches were real.

"Sorry," Harvey mumbled. "I only wanted to do something nice for Sabrina."

Tommy's hug was engulfing; Harvey pulled in roughly with Tommy's hand cupping the back of his head.

"You were pulling a dumb stunt, is what you were doing." Tommy pressed a kiss against the side of Harvey's head. "You big dope. This ends now, all right?"

"All right," Harvey answered in a small voice.

I stood helpless and silent, watching them, looking at my friends and the incongruously cheery line of flowers.

I'd almost moved to defend Harvey from Tommy, but I should've known better. I'd kept my secrets, and that had kept us all apart.

If we weren't witches, I would know Tommy well enough to understand him. If we weren't witches, Harvey and I would both know each other's families better. Harvey could come in and sit at our kitchen table, as I sometimes suspected he would like to. Aunt Hilda could fuss over him, and we wouldn't be afraid of letting out our secrets, because I wouldn't have any secrets from him.

His brother wasn't the one who had hurt Harvey. My cousin and I had done that.

Right now, I wished we weren't witches at all.

WHAT HAPPENS IN THE DARK

Zelda Spellman knows that Satan deserves her wholehearted devotion. She intends to give it.

She can allow no faltering on her dark and midnight path. But though Zelda tries to stride forward, obstacles are constantly placed in her way.

Witches live their long lives on the knife-edge of danger. The massacre in Salem and the other massacre, the one that happened in their own town, hang over the heads of every witch like a bright sword that will cut down all their glorious shadows. Witches starved in the ice and had to eat their own. Witch-hunters dared descend on a branch of her own family, the proud, ancient family of Spellmans, in England. If witch-hunters want to come for Zelda Spellman, they are more than welcome to try.

Zelda isn't afraid for herself at all.

People seem surprised to find that Zelda loves babies. Zelda has spent centuries wondering why people are such fools. She has received no answer on this subject as yet.

What's not to like about babies? Babies are splendid. Babies do not disappoint you or leave you. They have sweet-smelling heads, and plump, juicy flesh, and endless potential to serve Satan. Zelda is the finest midwife their coven has ever seen, and she often revels in the sin of pride because of it. A shame Hilda doesn't have half Zelda's gifts, Zelda often thinks smugly, while she is cuddling a new little darling for the Dark Lord after another triumphant birth.

It is a bitter irony that the appearance of the baby Zelda loves best brought tragedy. When her niece, Sabrina, was transported by magic away from the crash that killed her parents, Zelda had looked upon her adorable little face and known that Sabrina's father, their brother, Edward, the pride and joy of the family, was dead.

Sabrina's mother's family wanted to take her. Father Blackwood, the new head of the Church of Night, offered to take Sabrina in and raise her with the delightfully evil orphans in the Academy of Unseen Arts. Zelda cannot help admiring Father Blackwood's commitment to Satan, and also the trim figure he cuts in a brocade cloak. The Dark Lord has given Father Blackwood many gifts, including that of a sweet behind.

But Zelda said no to Father Blackwood. To Diana's family, she said, *Never approach Sabrina again or I will rip off your faces and you will die, faceless and screaming.* Hilda had to make Diana's family forget those threats, which is a pity as Zelda thought they were convincing and beautifully worded.

But then, Hilda's always been the weak and sentimental sister. Their brother, Edward, was so magnificent he could not be challenged, so certain that the Dark Lord spoke to him that everyone else believed that when Edward Spellman spoke, he did so in Satan's own voice.

Edward is gone. If Edward could be taken, any one of them could be.

Sometimes Zelda can only sleep because Hilda is resting in the bed next to her own, Hilda's even breathing her lullaby. Sometimes Zelda thinks it would be easier to be one of the coven's orphans. *I would die of loneliness,* she thinks the next moment, and then tells herself, no, she would be able to serve the Dark Lord with single-minded devotion.

She would die of loneliness. That's her secret. She is not the true servant of Satan the coven believes. She is an oath breaker and an abomination. She loves her family more than him.

But nobody ever has to know that.

Sometimes the lullaby of Hilda's breathing doesn't work, and Zelda has to creep up the stairs to the attic, to see Ambrose is alive. The wretched boy kicks off the covers and twists them, as if he is making hangmen's nooses or ropes to escape towers in his sleep. *Someone* has to straighten the covers out. Ambrose might catch a cold.

Hilda gallivanted off to England for ages and returned with a ridiculous boy in tow, which is so typical. Zelda highly disapproved of Ambrose from the first. He never listens, can't be trusted, can't be still. He's always laughing at her, and even when he isn't, it's like he is. He has those laughing eyes. He is her disgrace, her burden, her family's bad apple.

He is hers, and Zelda would kill anyone who tried to take him away.

It's a burning shame that Ambrose committed a crime and besmirched the family name, but Zelda thinks the punishment was very fitting. Satan guided the coven's hand there. Ambrose will be under Zelda's eye forever. It's better for him to stay home.

Next Zelda steals softly into Sabrina's room. There is never any need to straighten Sabrina's covers. She sleeps under the sheets on her back, flat as a corpse or a good girl. She hugs a big stuffed rabbit toy in her sleep. Zelda offered her a lovely real stuffed fox, but Sabrina said no. The silly girl doesn't know what's good for her. Zelda worries about that.

When Sabrina was little, Zelda would walk the floors by night carrying her. If Sabrina wanted to be held all night, that was fine with Zelda. Sabrina slept better when she was being held and rocked. Sabrina would clutch at people with her tiny fists when they tried to put her down, and her grip was amazingly strong. Zelda believes that Sabrina got that tenacity from her. Sabrina's not soft like Hilda, not unsteady like Ambrose. Zelda raised her and trained her to be the perfect witch.

These days, Sabrina is so close to her dark baptism. Zelda doesn't want to disturb her sleep.

After checking on Sabrina, Zelda goes outside and sits in a graceless way she would never permit anybody to see, and buries her face in her knees.

Oh sweet Satan, the shame if anybody ever did see. They would think she was weaker than Hilda.

When Zelda feels most insecure and irritable, she knows she kills Hilda too often. Kept safe under Spellman ground, Hilda can't leave her. If Zelda kills Hilda, for a few moments Zelda is certain nobody else can. And when Hilda crawls from the Cain Pit in front of their house, sometimes Zelda can pretend Edward will follow Hilda, and her sister and her brother will both come home.

Zelda knows she has to let Sabrina go out into the wide world of shadows waiting for her. Sabrina could be the pride and joy of the family reborn. Zelda wants that with terrible, clawing ferocity. She tries to crush out her fear for Sabrina, half mortal and wholly precious, her terror that Sabrina will be reckless, will be disobedient, will be lost. She tries to silence the voice inside her that screams Sabrina is in danger.

Sabrina's dark baptism will go perfectly. She will make Zelda proud.

Zelda feels sometimes as if her heart might break, but she knows her heart must not be divided.

KISSING THE MOON

I talked fast and convinced Principal Hawthorne that the flowers were an art project meant to celebrate Greendale.

"Like the fireworks at the Last Day of Summer fair."

Principal Hawthorne frowned. "I didn't know they had fireworks at the fair."

"Well, they did," I said. "Ask anyone. Harvey chose the school because—what better place than Baxter High to showcase civic pride? Right, Harvey?"

Harvey, a bad liar, flushed and muttered: "Right."

"That was some quick thinking in there, Sabrina," Tommy complimented me afterward, when we had gotten away with the promise that we would take down and clean up all the flowers ourselves. "Now Dad never has to know. But you and I will be talking about this later, Harvey."

Harvey hung his head. "Okay."

Harvey was not the only one subdued for the rest of the day. Susie and Roz weren't questioning me about Harvey's behavior. It had gone too far for that, I thought. They were truly unsettled, and instead of confronting what they could not altogether understand, they wanted to shove it behind us and pretend it hadn't happened.

I wished I could put it behind me, but the mortals had no idea who was responsible. I did.

I wouldn't let Harvey walk me home through the woods. I went home knowing that I had to have a serious talk with Ambrose.

Aunt Zelda was sitting in one of the rocking chairs on the far end of the porch, smoking. The sinking sun caught the gold of her cigarette holder, and the gold winked at me in time with the orange eye of her lit cigarette. "Sit with me a moment, Sabrina."

I hesitated, but I didn't particularly want to have a confrontation with Ambrose in the morgue, yelling over a corpse. Maybe I too welcomed the excuse to delay the moment for just a little while longer. I sank onto the rocking chair beside Aunt Zelda's and waited to hear what she had to say.

"I apologize if I have been short-tempered lately."

I almost fell out of my rocking chair. Aunt Zelda seldom apologized for anything.

"I know that I have been snapping at you, and making more frequent visits to the Church of Night, and occasionally—"

"Killing Aunt Hilda—"

"Yes, yes," said Aunt Zelda, rolling her eyes. "Small things, but I've noticed that you have been withdrawn these last couple of days. I know the months before you sign your soul over to the Dark Lord are a very special and sensitive time for a young girl. I fear I've been slightly inconsiderate, especially considering your special circumstances."

"Being half mortal, you mean," I said slowly. "You're worried that will make me weak."

Aunt Zelda said: "Of course that's a concern."

My heart kept rolling between resentment and guilt. Aunt Hilda being hurt, Aunt Zelda being worried: both were my fault, simply for being what I was. How was that fair?

"Other members of the Church of Night may doubt you," Aunt Zelda continued. "The thought of your heritage does make me nervous, but I want to assure you that I have complete faith in you. I am certain you will overcome the challenges posed by your background. I knew Edward better than anyone. He was a fantastically powerful warlock who inspired and amazed all those around him, and you are his daughter."

"I am. I want to be."

I did. But did that mean I couldn't be my mother's daughter at all?

If I didn't inspire and amaze all with my fantastical power, would I be a disappointment and a failure?

The sun was going down, the last light bleeding out of the sky. The landscape was already in shadow. The treetops were already black masses against gray clouds.

Aunt Zelda leaned away from me, causing her chair to rock back slightly. "I hope this little talk eases your mind, Sabrina. I don't want you to focus on anything but your dark baptism. I truly couldn't bear if any more shame was brought on our family."

"And that's your biggest concern?" I stood up. "Good to know."

The Church of Night doubted that I had the potential to be a witch. Maybe they were all like the Weird Sisters.

I could become a great witch and show them they were wrong. I could refuse to be a witch, and show them I didn't need them.

I wanted to do both. I felt like I was being pulled in two different directions, and nobody cared that I would be torn in half.

What I hadn't wanted to do before suddenly seemed the only choice.

✳✳✳

I stormed into the house and made my descent into the morgue, down the spiral stairs and through the cracked stone passageway. My flat shoes hit the black and white tiles hard.

Ambrose was almost finished with the work of the day. The steel table was empty, the cabinets in which bodies were kept on their cold shelves closed. Ambrose stood by the table under the stark fluorescent spotlight, taking off gloves and goggles. The air smelled of herbs and chemicals, and everything was gray and sharp-edged except for the single beam of light above his head.

"Tell me what the last words of the spell were," I ordered. I was panting as if I'd run a long way, through the woods in fear rather than down the stairs in my own house. "Tell me what you did to Harvey."

Ambrose shrugged, an irritable roll of his shoulders, as if he was actively trying to shrug a burden off.

"If I'd known you were going to make this much of a fuss about the silly spell, I'd never have suggested casting it with you. Read my lips, cousin. I'm not going to tell you. I don't feel like it, and I don't know why you're being such a killjoy lately. The whole purpose of magic is to make our lives more fun. Harvey's just—"

"Just *what?*" I bit out. "Just a mortal?"

A smile began to play along Ambrose's lips. Ambrose was always playing. "Well. Yes."

When I saw Harvey's blood on the ground, I'd thought for a moment I was seeing flowers. The light chime of my cousin's voice rang in my ears like bells. Even now, he thought this was a joke.

"Then what am I?"

The gloves Ambrose had taken off were lying crumpled on the steel table, still stained with blood. His hands were clean, and his brow was clear, entirely untroubled.

"Do you mean what are you in an existential sense? I find having philosophical conversations when sober very tiresome. I don't know what you are, cousin. What am I?"

"You're a criminal," I told him.

I'd never said anything like that to him before.

Ambrose's smile turned glittering and dangerous as his scalpel. "I'm the wicked witch of any direction you like. Sure."

The mortal world, the world I'd grown up in, was meaningless to him. Magic could hurt people, but Ambrose didn't care. Mortals were nothing to him, and perhaps I was nothing to him too.

"It wouldn't matter to you if your magic killed someone, would it?"

"Is there someone you want killed, cousin?" Ambrose inquired.

I hadn't thought I could get more angry.

"No, there isn't anyone I want killed!" I shouted. "And my name is Sabrina. Call me by my name. Mortals aren't playthings or possessions. Harvey's not one, and neither am I."

"I know Harvey isn't a possession," Ambrose said. "If he was, you'd get to keep him. You're not going to keep him, and I thought we both wanted to make your last few weeks with him more fun. You take things too seriously."

"You take things too lightly. These aren't my last few weeks with him. Am I really supposed to play with Harvey like he's a toy, and then throw him out like he's trash?"

Ambrose made a tiny gesture of dismissal. The steel lid of the trash flipped open. His crumpled, bloodstained gloves and gleaming scalpel flew through the air and disappeared inside. The lid clanged shut.

"Why not?" Ambrose drawled.

"Because witches have such cold, fickle hearts?" I whispered the words.

I hadn't wanted to believe them, but it seemed Ambrose had been telling the truth.

Ambrose shrugged. "There are a lot of reasons. I'm looking out for you here, cousin. I tried to tell you before. Witches and mortals, it never ends well. Know your witch history. Anne Boleyn married a mortal, and he cut her head off."

Ambrose drew a fingernail across his own throat with a dramatic sound effect.

"After your dark baptism, you'll understand. Do you know what they call flying, when witches do it? Kissing the moon. To be a witch is to kiss the moon," said Ambrose. "Ask yourself, would you rather kiss the moon, or him?"

His tone as he asked the question was cruel. The question itself was cruel.

"Why should I have to make the choice?" I demanded. "You really do think I should just abandon him, as if he isn't a person who matters to me. Is that why you always call me *cousin*? Because it doesn't matter who I am? Just the amusing half-mortal cousin, a baby who shouldn't have annoyed you by growing up."

Ambrose's lips skinned back from his teeth. "I have no idea why you believe you're so amusing. You were the one who insisted on playing with me when you were little, as if I was some kind of pet you kept indoors."

"That's right. Aunt Hilda and Aunt Zelda raised me, but you only played with me. I'm nothing but a toy to you."

Ambrose was encouraging me to discard Harvey and my mortal friends so easily. Was that what he would do to me if he could? When would I get thrown out like trash?

Ambrose cut his gaze from mine, eyes on the wall. The green tiles and dim lights of the mortuary made me feel as if we were not underground but underwater, with everything around me gone murky and unclear. Ambrose shrugged out of his bloodstained apron. Underneath he was wearing a worn T-shirt bearing the words GREEN MEANS GO. RED MEANS GO FASTER. The T-shirt was red as blood and roses.

Ambrose actually laughed, though the sound was strained. "Why are you taking this so personally?"

I took an enraged step forward. "Because it's personal! Because my parents were a witch and a mortal."

"Well, Sabrina," said Ambrose coolly. "They didn't live happily ever after, did they? You have to live to do that."

I crossed the floor of the morgue in two strides. My hand flew out to slap him, but Ambrose caught my wrist. I fought to get free and hit him, but Ambrose held on, fingers biting into my skin.

"You're pathetic," I spat at him. "You're jealous of me because I have a life and you don't. Are you going to deny it?"

"I'm not. I *am* jealous," Ambrose snarled back. "If I had a chance at a life, I'd live it a hundred times better than you!"

"So you did a spell that would hurt Harvey because you want to ruin my life, and you don't care how many mortals you hurt to do it?"

The ring of white around Ambrose's eyes was broader than it was for other people. Now his wide, strange eyes were almost rolling inside his head, black and white and furious. It had never occurred to me before that my cousin could be sinister, or threatening.

Not to me.

"Why not?" he asked softly. "Your precious mortals can rot for all I care. I don't know why you're obsessed with them, but you never think about the fact that I live in a cage!"

I broke his hold on my wrist with a violent wrench. "This isn't a cage. This is our home. You never think about what it means to me to be half mortal."

"It doesn't matter that you're half mortal. Your dark baptism is in a month," said Ambrose. "You will write your name in the Dark Lord's book, and then you'll be as bad a witch as any of them. Or is that the problem, Sabrina? You're not really desperately concerned about the mortals. You're as selfish as I am. You're worried about yourself, and the fact you're going to fail."

My voice couldn't shake, so I made it steely. "And why would you think that?"

Ambrose seemed only too happy to fill me in. He swung away from me, prowling toward the steel table, but I shoved myself between him and the table. I made him look at me, and he bent down and said the malicious, vicious words to my face.

"You wear hairbands to bed, Sabrina. Some of them match your pajamas. You're like the girl in one of our stories who swore to a witch she would touch no evil and ended up with no hands. You march around wearing your hairbands like a crown, peering out from underneath at a world you don't understand but can't stop judging. The only thing I can imagine you doing with the Dark Lord is telling him sternly that you're disappointed in his naughty behavior. What kind of witch will you be?"

You're such a good girl. Sometimes I wonder how you're ever going to make a wicked witch. He'd said that to me before we ever did the spell on Harvey. I'd grown up believing that one day I would be a witch, with a grimoire of my own like my cousin's, that I would do spells and be as splendid as my cousin, but this was what witches really were. Witches had cold, fickle hearts. Ambrose didn't believe in me, and he didn't care about me.

"I'll be a better witch than *you*," I swore to Ambrose. "It's not my fault you're trapped in here with me. You committed a crime decades before I was born! You're weak, you did wrong, and you ruined your own life. You deserve to be in a cage."

"You don't deserve to be a witch!" shouted Ambrose. "That's what you keep thinking, isn't it? You can't bear that little whisper of doubt in your head, so you try to crush it out. I wasn't the one who wanted to cast spells to make certain of a boyfriend. You're angry because you're afraid that you're even more weak and pathetic than me."

His eyes were furious in the dim green light. His words sounded like a curse, as if by saying the words he could make them true.

My hands were curled in fists so tight my hands ached. "This is stupid. I'm done listening to you."

"Yeah?" Ambrose's laugh curled in the air, wicked and mocking, the cackle of a true witch. "Well, I'm done with you."

My chest felt as if it was a nest of snakes, coiling and writhing and striking at my insides with sharp fangs. I lifted my fists and saw that Ambrose's hands, hanging by his sides, were clenched. I could hear the steel trays moving in the cabinets, the empty ones rattling, the ones with corpses inside rocking as if they were boughs holding babies that must break. Even the sea-green tiles and the bricks in the walls were shifting. In a few moments this ringing room would be full of scalpels and the dead.

There came the sound of high heels on the spiral stairs, striking so violently I thought sparks might fly.

"Children!" Aunt Zelda thundered. "What in Satan's name do you think you're playing at?"

Ambrose's voice was flat. "We're not playing."

"Sibling rivalry," Aunt Hilda murmured, hovering uneasily behind Zelda on the stairs. "It...it's natural, it happens, I've read about it in child psychology books—"

"What nonsense you talk," snapped Aunt Zelda. "Cease reading mortal drivel. There's obviously a perfectly rational explanation. They have probably been possessed by demons."

My shout sliced through the noise of my aunts bickering.

"How would it be sibling rivalry? He's not my brother. We're nothing to each other. This isn't a *real* family."

I recoiled from Ambrose, stalked past my hurt and offended aunts, whirled up both sets of stairs to my bedroom, hurled myself on the bed full of stupid stuffed toys and tasseled pillows, and burst into a bitter storm of tears.

Aunt Zelda only cared about me not shaming the Spellmans. Even Aunt Hilda wouldn't take my side over Ambrose. And Ambrose was done with me, a toy who had ceased to be amusing, so I was done with him.

If witches didn't even love each other, there was no reason to be a witch.

WHAT HAPPENS IN THE DARK

A witch's words can travel far on the right wind. They race from leaf to leaf in the woods like a game of whispers. It is an old legend that the rustling of fallen leaves around a house means witches are gossiping about the family who lives within.

Tommy Kinkle is out on his porch, leaning against the rail and looking out into the deep woods. He wonders what Harvey would see if his baby brother the artist were standing beside him. Fairies, maybe? Tommy himself just sees trees. He's a straightforward kind of guy.

Harvey came home still babbling about Sabrina, as if he didn't see her every day all day. Kid's a trip. But Dad didn't go to the bar or pass out early tonight. Dad's glowering in front of the TV with a beer, so Harvey went to his room, saying he was going to draw something. Maybe Dad will drop off to sleep soon, and Harvey will venture outside. Tommy hopes so. Talking with Harvey is the best part of his day.

Harvey's right to stay out of Dad's path. Dad has a heavy hand and a bad temper when he's been drinking. He's hit Tommy a few times, but Tommy is strong enough to take it. Dad has never hit Harvey, and he's not going to. If Dad beat Tommy to death and then raised a hand to Harvey, Tommy would rise from his grave to catch it.

He's good at catching, good at goals; he's the determined type. Everyone at school back in the day knew that: quarterback Tommy, he'll make the touchdown. You can count on Tommy Kinkle. Coach used to say, *This game is the fight of your lives!* It's the same in the mines now. When the other guys are shrinking back or murmuring about getting the creeps, when it's close and dark and hot as hell, when he remembers little Harvey telling him a wild, terror-stricken story about seeing a demon in the mines, Tommy leads the way.

Once when they were both small, they went to a fun fair. Harvey got stuck in the Hall of Mirrors, scared of his own reflection transforming into a monster he couldn't recognize. Tommy busted right into that place. He didn't even notice the reflections: He saw only his scared kid brother. He only knew that he was getting Harvey out.

Tommy doesn't have much imagination. He believes what he sees, and he knows what's real. It's Harvey who got the imagination and the nerves, Harvey who got their mama's dark eyes and her tragic mouth. Tommy was born a good old boy. His dad and his gramps both call him *my boy Tommy*, they both understand him—there's not much to understand, Tommy thinks—but they don't understand Harvey, and it makes them edgy.

It's up to Tommy to understand Harvey, or try to, now their mama is gone. Harvey tells Tommy all his secrets. He whispered to Tommy, on his first day of school, that he'd met a girl who looked like a princess, and every day since then he'd come home with another tale of Princess Sabrina. When Harvey was little, he cried on the frequent days when their dad and grandpa went hunting, and asked didn't Tommy feel awful for the poor deer? Tommy hadn't thought about it before, but once Harvey said it, Tommy could see it. The deer have his baby brother's eyes, big and brown and too easily hurt.

Hunting is a Kinkle tradition. Gramps says their family legacy is the blood they were strong enough to spill, and the darkness of the mines. They have never forgiven Harvey for being born a gentle soul.

"Oh, Harvey's sensitive all right," their dad sneered once when they were down in the mines. "All his friends are girls, and he loves drawing pretty pictures. He'd better not be too sensitive, if you know what I'm sayin'."

Tommy had barked out a genuinely startled laugh. "Are you kidding, Dad? All he thinks about is Sabrina."

His dad's mouth is perpetually disappointed, moving from bitter shape to bitter shape. "The Spellman girl. Can't stand the Spellmans. They're real strange folks."

The Spellmans might be strange. People say they are: that Hilda is daft, Zelda is an old witch, and the cousin is a sinner.

There are a lot of strange things in Greendale, and a lot of Greendale people who get scared by what they can't understand. Tommy's not one of them.

He started going to Harvey's parent-teacher meetings a couple of years back. His dad wouldn't go to them, had no interest. It was weird to return to school, where Tommy had walked the halls a king not so long ago. Everybody had wanted to be his friend then, wanted a word or a nod from him, and it was the same building but now he was sitting lined up on the rickety chairs with a bunch of parents in their best clothes, waiting to talk to the principal. His head was hanging, his hands clasped awkwardly together, and the dust from the mines was still on his boots. It felt as if he was in trouble, and hopelessly out of place. He'd almost walked right out.

But Hilda Spellman was there, Sabrina's aunt with the

butter-yellow hair and the kind face. She'd been reading a book, held open in her lap. Tommy's high school girlfriend used to read a lot too. Tommy was no great reader himself, but it gave him kind of a nice feeling to see people with books: getting away from Greendale in their own minds. He hadn't been surprised to see Hilda with a book. The Spellmans had that look about them: smart women. A cut above. *They think they're better than us mere mortals,* his dad says.

Hilda Spellman had shoved her book in her purse and waved him over, chatted to him until it was their turn to talk to the teachers.

"It's nice to have you here," she whispered to him. "I always feel uneasy, being the only one who isn't a parent, and Zelda won't come with me." She gave him a little friendly wink, her bright blue eye shadow flickering at him. "We're all doing the best we can, eh?"

Tommy had cleared his throat. "Yeah."

When he talked to the teachers, they told him Harvey was doing pretty good in class, though he was absentminded.

"That's my little brother," said Tommy ruefully. "He's a dreamer."

Harvey doesn't think he's smart, but Tommy knows he is. And whenever he went to parent-teacher meetings from then on, Tommy sat by Hilda Spellman. She always smiled when she saw him, took the time to talk. She was a real lady.

One night, Tommy was worried about Harvey being out late. Harvey'd said he'd be at the Spellman house, and Tommy walked up through the woods under the cover of darkness. He saw the porch of the Spellman house lit up and the silhouettes of a boy and girl sitting there. He didn't want to disturb Harvey's courting, but he did need to fetch Harvey back, so he'd approached quietly.

It hadn't been Harvey sitting on the porch with Sabrina. It had been Sabrina's cousin, Ambrose.

People in town talked a lot about the cousin. Every woman who'd ever delivered the mail to the Spellman house was a little in love with him. So were a few of the mailmen. He flirted with them all, everybody said, like it just didn't matter. But he never asked to take anyone out, so they knew he didn't mean it.

He was cold and cruel, Tommy'd heard. A playboy as well as a sinner.

But Tommy didn't know about that. Maybe Ambrose Spellman was just too big a personality for Greendale. Sometimes you saw him, pacing the boundaries of the Spellman lands like a caged panther in a fancy dressing gown, flinging his arms out wide as if to embrace the four winds. Sometimes you didn't see him for months on end, and Tommy figured at those times Ambrose went away on glamorous, outlandish journeys. He didn't look much older than Tommy was himself, but he must be older than he seemed: The stories about him went way back, and you could tell just by looking at him that he'd had a thousand wild adventures, and small-town life would never be enough for him. Tommy figured Ambrose Spellman was probably the coolest guy Greendale would ever see: No wonder they didn't understand him.

That night, Ambrose was talking to Sabrina in a deep, dream-laden voice. He had an English accent, as Hilda Spellman did. They'd spent enough time in England that they had actual English accents: Tommy'd never even gotten a passport, and doubted he ever would, but he looked some-times at maps of strange lands, and thought Ambrose Spellman had probably been to them all. Ambrose was gesturing as he talked, and he wore a bracelet—Tommy could only picture his father's reaction if Tommy ever lost his mind and decided to wear a bracelet, but it was clear Ambrose didn't care what anybody thought.

He was telling Sabrina a story, something about witches and magic and deep woods and a long past. Ambrose talked as if it was really true, and Sabrina answered as if it was true as well. Hilda came out on the porch with hot chocolates for them both, and she joined the conversation too, speaking eas-ily as though from long habit. It was clear they were used to spinning magic stories for each other. Maybe, Tommy thought, Ambrose was a writer, maybe he wrote fantasy books like Tommy's girl Martha used to read: that would make sense of the swaggering around in silk dressing gowns and the, uh, bohemian lifestyle. Writers were different from other folks. Everybody knew that.

Tommy's mother died when he and his brother were young enough that she still told them stories, and Tommy had no idea that people grew out of storytelling. Motherless children are easy prey for witches.

Tommy wasn't suspicious. He just liked listening to the boy's voice, weaving a tale of magic for his cousin. It sounded like family.

Tommy stayed for longer than he should have, so entirely charmed that he forgot it wasn't neighborly to spy. He stayed until Sabrina fell asleep, her golden head on her cousin's silk-clad shoulder, and Ambrose stopped talking.

Insects flew toward Sabrina's small, curled-up sleeping form. Ambrose gave a lordly wave, and the insects flew off: not just the ones he'd swept at, but every insect on the porch cleared out instantly. As if that protective little gesture, which Tommy found so sweet, had been real magic.

Only a single firefly stayed. When Ambrose lifted his hand, the tiny lantern of the firefly landed on his finger, shining there.

"Light my cousin's dreams," he whispered.

What a strange, pretty thing to say, Tommy thought: What a sweetheart. He didn't believe a word of what people said about the Spellmans, not a word.

Ambrose fell asleep too, his dark head drooping against Sabrina's, and their aunt came out and covered them with a blanket. Not the nice one, Hilda, but Zelda Spellman, who wielded a cigarette holder shaped like a pitchfork as if she might just stab somebody's eyes out. She covered the cousins up carefully, tucking the quilt under their chins and around their feet, but she also surveyed the darkness with a suspicious glare, and Tommy finally remembered that he should leave.

Tommy found out that Harvey had been fibbing about being at the Spellmans' house because Susie and Roz had drama class, and Harvey was walking Sabrina home, then doubling back to walk with Susie and Roz. There were boys at school who were unkind to Susie, saying she was hardly a girl at all. Their father laughed at Susie for the same reason.

"I didn't want to tell Dad," Harvey confessed. "And I didn't want Sabrina finding out about the boys annoying Susie and Roz on their way back from drama. She'd go wild, Tommy! And she has to be back home, you know. Her aunt Zelda teaches her Latin after school. Sabrina speaks Latin, can you believe?"

Harvey shone whenever he talked about her. He thought Sabrina could do just about anything. Of course, that was the impression Sabrina usually gave. Greendale people, when they were doing their whispering, said Sabrina was a little know-it-all. Tommy could absolutely picture Sabrina giving schoolboys hell for annoying her friends.

But Harvey didn't want Sabrina worried, and Tommy doubted that Harvey on his own would be enough to stop the boys harassing his friends. Harvey thought fighting was ugly, and Tommy's artistic brother couldn't bear ugliness.

Tommy didn't like it himself, but he could bear it. He walked Harvey, Roz, and Susie home the next day, and when the other boys saw Tommy there, they didn't dare approach. Tommy's football legend, fading every day, was good for that, at least.

"Don't you worry about them, Susie," Roz said energetically. "In a few years, you'll be living in a big city, and those jerks will be rotting in Greendale as hometown has-beens!"

Her dark eyes, behind their big spectacles, had darted to Tommy as soon as she'd spoken. Roz might wear those huge glasses, but she saw plenty.

"I didn't mean . . ." she began.

"'Course you didn't," Harvey said stoutly. "Tommy's not a jerk. And he was an all-star!"

His little brother was proud of him now, but Harvey might be embarrassed by him one day. Roz wasn't wrong. Tommy's dad had an album of his own pictures, as well as Tommy's, showing him playing football, being a hometown hero who came to nothing. Nobody cared about those crumbling photos now, except for Tommy's dad, and someday soon nobody would care about Tommy's pictures either. It was strange, knowing that his best days were behind him, when he was barely in his twenties.

It was what it was. Tommy did try not to be a jerk.

Back in school, people had said he could have any girl he wanted. Tommy didn't know about that, but a few cheerleaders had made it clear they were available. That hadn't mattered. Tommy'd had a steady girl all through high school. He'd gotten to know Martha when they did a project for extra credit, and she'd seemed surprised when he did his share of the work, though he didn't have the extra creative spark Martha did. Tommy liked the way her eyes went sweet and dreamy over a book. He guessed doing his share won him extra credit with Martha. She'd said yes when he asked her out, though she'd looked surprised as some other people in school had, and they went steady for three years. She would come back to Tommy's place sometimes and help Harvey with his homework. Harvey liked her almost as much as Tommy did.

Tommy had asked Martha to marry him when they graduated. He wasn't surprised when she said no. They both knew she was meant for bigger, shinier things than the little diamond ring that was all he'd been able to afford even after taking on extra shifts at the mines. He'd asked her to keep the ring and think about him sometimes when she was in the big city. She had kept the ring, but she hadn't kept in touch.

Maybe Martha's answer would've been different if he'd taken the football scholarship. Tommy had been offered a free ride to a great college. He'd thought about taking it. Martha had thought he was crazy not to. Harvey would never have blamed him. But Tommy would've blamed himself.

Whenever he thought about his own future, Tommy saw it looping back to living and dying in Greendale. He could go off and pretend for a while, but he didn't have what Martha and Harvey and Sabrina did, the extra spark that would power them out of this town. He was scared of proving what he already knew deep down was true: He didn't have what it took. He might blow his knee out and it would all be for nothing, and even if he didn't . . .

Leaving meant leaving Harvey alone at home, with their dad. It meant Tommy miles away, not there to take their father's blows and the brunt of his disappointment with life. Harvey's sensitive spirit, being crushed.

"Take this," their mama had said when she was dying, pressing a bright cross into Tommy's hands and bundling

Harvey into his arms. "Take him. Promise me you'll take care of your brother."

Tommy tried to speak with dignity, though he was young and frightened. He knew the promise was sacred. He said: "Yes, ma'am."

He turned down the free ride to college. He stayed in Greendale where he belonged.

It's not that Tommy doesn't have his own dreams, but he knows it's better this way. He didn't really want Martha staying in town, her eyes growing as sad as his mother's. He hopes that she looks at the ring now and again, and that the memory of him is sweet: the boy back home who treated her right and knew her worth when some fools did not. He'd rather that than if she'd stayed, and her thoughts of him turned bitter.

It was the same with Alison, the girl with the golden hair and green coat who picked Tommy up in the bar and talked about going away to LA together. She hadn't been kind like Martha, but gosh, she'd been pretty, eyes shining like faraway city lights. It was sweet, to sit with her in her tiny hotel room and talk and dream, but Tommy knew he wasn't going anywhere. One day, when the photographs in his album had faded a little more, he wouldn't be the boy a pretty girl picked on her way out of town. He'd just be one more of the good old boys at the bar, talking about the good old days and the good old dreams.

Tommy hopes Alison reached LA and found it everything she dreamed. Tommy will never know that she is dead, lost beneath dark waters, never to leave this town.

Tommy tried to talk to Harvey the way he'd heard Ambrose speak to Sabrina, once. He'd faltered out a few sentences about witches and dragons, but in Tommy's mouth none of it sounded convincing. Harvey had looked badly worried. He'd asked Tommy not to start drinking like Dad, and Tommy swallowed and swore he wouldn't.

When his dad said the Spellmans were strange, Tommy remembered Hilda Spellman at the parent-teacher meetings, remembered that night with Ambrose Spellman telling stories and talking to a firefly, and he said: "I think the Spellmans are real nice folks. I'm glad Harvey knows them."

His father grunted. "Better than if Harvey was seeing that Walker girl, or that other girl who acts like a boy, I suppose. That would be as bad as if he *was* that way!"

Tommy cleared his throat and said: "If Harvey was that way... there ain't nothing wrong with it."

Dad's face went grim. He'd swung his pick down and broken a stone in half, and said: "I'd rather see my boy dead."

A guy asked Tommy out, once. Not Sabrina's cousin—Ambrose doesn't know Tommy is alive—it was a blond guy Tommy didn't know. Tommy was in Cerberus Books, trying to hunt up a book on art that Harvey wanted, when the guy approached him. Tommy said no, obviously. He was as nice as he knew how to be about it, even while he was looking around in panic to see if anyone his dad knew could hear. Tommy didn't like the look of the guy or anything, not at all, but he was impressed the blond guy had the nerve to ask him. Even in Greendale, some people were brave. They lived their lives in a small town as if they knew they were going to get out.

Maybe Sabrina's wild writer cousin talks to Harvey sometimes, tells him wonderful stories he makes sound true. Tommy hopes so.

If Ambrose has, Harvey hasn't mentioned it, but then, whenever the conversation turns to the Spellmans, he only talks about Sabrina. She's about all he sees, and it's not hard to see why. Sabrina shines, not like city lights but like a sun. Tommy worries about Harvey and his other friends, but he never worries about Sabrina walking through the woods.

Light my cousin's dreams.

That girl carries her family's love with her like a steady flame, a warm light encircling her golden head and making a bright path for her feet to follow without faltering. She's a little bit of a thing, but she strides tall and fearless as her cousin, speaks with the authority of Zelda Spellman, and is kind to her friends as Hilda Spellman was to Tommy. Sabrina would walk confidently into the deepest dark or the wildest adventure. Tommy wishes he had that certainty. He'd give it to Harvey, who doesn't walk like Sabrina does, who shies away like a scared animal sometimes when people get close. But Harvey always walks by Sabrina's side. Perhaps Sabrina will be sure of Harvey as she is of most things, sure as nobody has ever been about Tommy. Perhaps she can see in Harvey the greatness that Tommy can. Perhaps she will take Harvey with her, wherever she's going.

That's all Tommy wants. That's what Tommy intends to do with his life.

A tap comes, his little brother knocking on the open door of the Kinkle house, trying to get Tommy's attention.

"What are you doing, Tommy?"

Tommy shrugged. "Daydreaming, I guess."

Harvey's shy face brightened. "What are you dreaming about?"

"What do you think?" Tommy ruffled his hair. "I'm dreaming that all your dreams come true, nerd."

Harvey grinned as if Tommy was making a joke. "Do you want to see my drawing?"

"I sure do," said Tommy. "Let's have a preview before your pictures get put in the art galleries. I'll be right in. And hey, tomorrow? You need to talk to your girl."

Harvey bit his lip, nodded, then ran inside to set up the picture. He was glowing with pride. Harvey doesn't shine with Sabrina's certainty, but there's light there, even if it pales or flickers. He's the brightest thing in Tommy's life.

Reverend Walker says, in his sermons of blood and thunder and hellfire: *What would you do if you fell into the Pit?* The answer came to Tommy quick as winking. If Harvey was in the Pit with him, he'd have Harvey up on his shoulders fast as he could. Tommy has strong shoulders, and sure hands. He'd make sure Harvey got out.

Out of the room where their mother lay dying, out of the Hall of Mirrors, out of the enclosing shadows of Greendale.

This is the fight of your lives! Coach used to say about every game, but Tommy knew better then and he knows better now. Football is a game. This, Harvey, getting his baby brother out, is the fight of his life. Tommy made all his touchdowns, Tommy took every hit. Gramps says insistently that they have to be hunters, so Tommy taught Harvey to shoot better than Tommy himself can, but he won't let them make Harvey kill. When they're out hunting Tommy picks up the gun and fires at the deer so Harvey won't have to, and Tommy hits them between the eyes every time. Tommy works the longest shifts, down in the darkest parts of the mines, trying to get his dad to shut up about Harvey taking a shift. Harvey's not going down there. Harvey's only going up. Tommy will make it happen. He promised his mother. He's never failed yet. You can count on Tommy Kinkle. Everybody knows that.

Through the green trees that surround their small green house comes a rippling wind. It almost sounds like a voice, almost sounds like Sabrina's aunt Hilda, that kind woman. It's ridiculous that anybody calls her a witch.

In a house with no mother, where a cold man rules, a child pays.

"Let it be me," said Tommy Kinkle, letting go of the porch rail with a small sigh.

He'll pay: every day of his future, every drop of sweat and blood, every dream.

But not Harvey. Not his little brother. He's the best of their family, and Tommy is going to save him.

WITCHCRAFT IN YOUR LIPS

I woke to a flat, gray morning and dragged myself out of bed with my limbs aching almost as much as my eyes. I'd cried myself to sleep last night. The time on my porcelain clock was too early for this nonsense. When I looked into my mirror, I flinched, and I wasn't sure if that was because my mirror frame was decorated with painted white roses or because of the deep shadows under my eyes.

I told myself not to be silly, then put on a red dress and fixed a black hairband in place. Then I stared at myself in the mirror, tore the hairband out of my hair, and threw it down on my dressing table with a clatter. It spun in a dark circle and fell off the dressing table. I stood up, then bit my lip, dived for the hairband, and jammed it onto my head without checking the mirror to see how it looked.

I went downstairs in an extremely bad mood. Aunt Hilda jumped when I came in, and dropped her spoon. She'd made porridge, but by the smell and the thin, sad stream of smoke issuing from the pot, she'd burned it.

Aunt Zelda was having her breakfast cigarette at the table, but Ambrose wasn't there. He usually made sure to be downstairs to eat breakfast with me before I went to school, even if he'd stayed up on his laptop all night. I'd never thought about that much before.

I grabbed a bowl, sank down across the table from Aunt Zelda, and crunched resentfully on the burned bits in my porridge.

"You've burned the newt's eyeballs, Hilda," Aunt Zelda remarked critically. "Newt eyeballs should be al dente."

I choked on one of the … no, don't think it … pieces of burned porridge, then pushed my bowl away. I got up to get cereal, but Ambrose must have finished the box. I slammed the door of the cupboard shut.

"You should have something for breakfast," Aunt Hilda encouraged me.

"Okay," I said. "Aunt Z., can I have a cigarette?"

"Certainly not," Aunt Zelda snapped. "Cigarettes are extremely harmful for mortals. While I am doing homage to my lord Satan by accustoming myself to the smoke that will doubtless accompany the flames of hell."

She didn't have the subdued air that Aunt Hilda did, but she'd smoked about five cigarettes before breakfast. I wondered if she was thinking about me bringing shame on the family.

"I'm not a mortal," I snapped. "But I guess I'm close enough, right?"

Apparently my lungs were going to change after my dark baptism, as well as my soft mortal's heart.

"Don't say such things, or I'll wash your mouth out with holy water," threatened Aunt Zelda.

"Go ahead!"

"Don't test me!" Aunt Zelda put down her cigarette holder with a determined click. "This is absurd. I'm fetching Ambrose downstairs."

"I don't want to see him!" I called after her as she swept out. Aunt Zelda ignored me.

We listened to her climb both sets of stairs, toward the attic. Aunt Zelda's raised tones of command, and the angry rumble of Ambrose's responses. He wasn't coming downstairs. I saw Aunt Hilda let out her breath in a small, disappointed sigh at the same time I did.

I was furious with myself the next moment. He was done with me, and I was done with him. That meant no more getting up for breakfast before I went to school. It would mean no more holding the door wide for me when I came home from school, before I had a chance to open it myself, or waiting for me on the porch.

I shoved my chair back from the table and stood. "I'm sick of this."

"What if you go up and have a chat with Ambrose, eh, my love?" Aunt Hilda suggested.

I grabbed my book bag and my red coat. "I don't want to talk to him, and he doesn't want to talk to me."

I couldn't stay in the house another minute.

The Weird Sisters were lingering just outside the borders of our property. That was all I needed. Their shadows fell on me, shoulders hunched as if already laughing at my expense. They looked like a little flock of ravens perched up on a branch and sneering down on everyone who passed by.

"Good morrow, *not* sister," Prudence called out.

My voice was stony. "What do you want?"

"Just wanted to get the worst part of my day over with early," answered Prudence. "My, don't you look cheerful this morning. The mortals believe witches turn milk sour, but maybe that story started because of your face. How will I ever bear it when you're casting a blight on our academy?"

The cold morning breeze was in my eyes, making them water. I wiped at them roughly with the red cuff of my coat. "Maybe you won't have to find out," I snapped, and shouldered roughly past Prudence, leaving them squawking behind me. "Maybe I don't want to go."

I couldn't be bothered with them. Not today. They could get their kicks tormenting someone else.

Around the curve in the road, beneath the arch of trees beginning to die, I met Harvey walking up the road to my house.

✳✳✳

His eyes went wide, as startled to see me as I was to see him. He was wearing his jacket with one of the sheepskin-lined flaps tucked inside rather than outside, his hair ruffled even more than usual. He looked still sleepy, and worried, and entirely dear, and I couldn't face him right now.

"Hey, 'Brina. Where are you going?"

I cleared my throat. "To school. Early. I thought I'd go to school early."

"You weren't waiting for me?" Harvey swallowed this information. "I guess you're mad at me after all."

"No," I whispered. "I'm not mad."

I didn't want him thinking that. But he dipped his chin, accepting the responsibility that didn't belong to him.

"You have every right to be," Harvey said. "Tommy told me that I should talk to you. Can I?"

"I'm really not mad," I insisted. "You have no need to apologize. I should be the one—"

"Let me say this," Harvey said. "Please, 'Brina. It's important to me. I don't talk to you about my home life a lot."

That was my fault too. If I were a mortal, we'd both talk about our home lives more. Guilt and silence like ashes in my mouth, all I could do was nod, and let Harvey take my hand and draw me off the path, so we were standing under the low-hanging golden leaves and gray skies of early morning. All I could do was listen.

"The reason I don't tell you..." Harvey was the one who'd wanted to talk, but he seemed to find it hard to speak. He swallowed and struggled on. "It's not that I don't trust you. It's that I don't like thinking about it. When I'm at school, when I'm with you and Roz and Susie, I can pretend that everything is okay. I can feel normal."

It took an effort to speak, with my mouth so dry. "I can understand that."

Harvey gave me a tiny smile. "I hate it at home," he confessed. "My dad doesn't like me. My gramps is just like him, but more so. All they do is talk about being miners and hunters, being strong men. They think there's only one way to be strong, and I'm not it, and I think it makes them want to— break me, so they can remake me in a different shape. One that will please them more."

Fury rushed on me, red as blood. I was a witch, and if

anyone threatened what was mine, I would bring ruin. "You don't mean—"

Harvey shook his head quickly. "No, I don't. My dad doesn't hurt me or anything. He—yells, sometimes. He has a bad temper. But it's not like that. It's just whenever I'm at home, it's like I'm a stranger who came by. Someone he has nothing in common with, and he doesn't know why I'm there and he wants me to leave. I don't talk to you about it, because I want you to think I'm—stronger than I am, and cooler than I am. My dad doesn't want me. I guess I was afraid that if you knew that, then school wouldn't be an escape anymore, and you might start to wonder why he feels that way."

I squeezed his hands. "I don't have to wonder. Anyone who doesn't appreciate you is an idiot."

On my first day of school, I'd been so excited and so nervous to be among the mortals. Every single one of the other kids was taller than me back then, and Harvey was one of the tallest. I picked him out right away. While I was standing on tiptoes and craning my neck to try to make myself bigger, he was hunching his shoulders and ducking his head, trying to make himself look smaller. I pushed through the crowd, walked right up to him and took his hand, and he gave me a shy, delighted smile.

I'd liked him and Roz and Susie instantly, so much, but I

liked Harvey the best. And from the very beginning, I wanted him to like me best too. I'd cast this stupid spell because I wanted to have that certainty in my life, because I was still hoping he would like me the best of anyone.

I had always appreciated him. I could say that much for myself. But I shouldn't have done it.

"Do you remember the girl in the green coat, who we saw on the path through the woods?" Harvey asked. "I *was* watching her."

I nodded, because I knew that much. I'd cast the spell that got him hurt because I was insecure about not having all his attention.

"You made a joke about me looking at her because she was pretty," said Harvey. "I knew you couldn't really believe that I'd ever look at another girl, not in that way. I figured you might have an idea about what was actually happening, but I didn't want to tell you, just like I didn't want to tell you about what it's like at home. I didn't want to make it more real."

Harvey took a deep breath. I stared at him in utter confusion.

"The girl's name was Alison," he told me. "She was a tourist, on her way somewhere more exciting than the town she'd come from, and more exciting than Greendale. Only she met Tommy in a bar and decided to stick around. I wasn't eavesdropping on them, but I did overhear them talking the few times he brought her home. She wanted him to go with her, to Los Angeles. She talked about how amazing their new lives would be."

There was a silence. I think I would have been able to hear a leaf fall on the grass between us. I'd thought Harvey's family situation couldn't be as complicated as mine, not when his family was mortal and at least one of his parents was alive. I'd been blaming everything on my family being witches. I'd been wrong.

"I know you and your family don't care much about football. Honestly, neither do I, but—Tommy was captain of the Baxter High Ravens, a few years back. He was the quarterback, like Dad used to be, but Dad says that Tommy was better than he ever was. Tommy had a real gift.

"I was always sure that Tommy would get a football scholarship to a good college and be able to get out of Greendale. Go on to have a real future, something bigger and better than working in the family mines." Harvey gave a slight shudder as he mentioned the mines. "I would have missed him like hell. Tommy's the one person in my family who feels like my family. Mom died when I was too small to remember her properly. Tommy was always everything Dad and Gramps wanted him to be. He could've ignored me or despised me like they did. But he didn't. He played ball with me when I was a kid, and never cared that I wasn't good. He bought me my first sets of coloring pencils and paints, and still tells me every picture I draw is amazing. He was always bigger and stronger, and he used that to make me feel safe. Nobody ever had a better brother. I was so afraid of him leaving me alone."

"I know you really love him," I said quietly.

Harvey hesitated for a moment before he nodded, and plunged ahead with his tale.

"I don't know why nobody offered Tommy a football scholarship, but they didn't. He wasn't able to go to college. He had a high school girlfriend who was sweet and smart, and I know he loved her a lot, but she wouldn't stay in Greendale with him. She left and never came back. She never even called. He had to stay and live in our house and work in the mines. I know how unhappy and how trapped Tommy must have felt. I don't know what I'd do, if I thought I'd have to live that way forever. He never complains. He always acts like he's fine with everything. But suddenly he was dating this new girl, and she was really glamorous, and she was talking to Tommy about a way out. I thought he would take it. I knew there was no reason for him to stay."

"That's why you were so quiet and unhappy last week," I murmured. "That's why you looked at that girl. Because you knew her."

I'd been such a fool.

Harvey's face was like the sky, wide open with no way to hide either its darkness or its light. He was clearly miserable. "That girl, Alison, she's gone. Tommy said he wouldn't leave with her, so she left without him. He came home after the last time he met her, less than an hour after we saw her in the woods, and I just knew. He looked so unhappy, and I was mad at myself for being scared and dumb. He has a right to his own life. He should be happier than he is now. Instead he stayed in Greendale, and I know he stayed for me. He shouldn't have done it."

"He's your brother," I told Harvey. "If he stayed, he wants to. It means he loves you a lot."

I was almost jealous of that love, the way I had been before, considering the difference between Tommy and Ambrose.

We stood under the trees of dying summer with our hands clasped palm to palm. Thorns had sliced open Harvey's hands yesterday, the artist's hands I loved, and it was my fault. Today he was confessing, as if it was a sin that he'd been scared of losing his brother, and it broke my heart. I refused to be jealous of Harvey. I wanted him to have everything, love and kindness and constant protection. He deserved it all.

Harvey shook his head, obviously still doubtful. The wind pushed his untidy hair back with invisible fingers as if it loved him and wanted to see his face more clearly. He never cut his hair often enough, and it had never occurred to me before now that he didn't have a mother, or aunts, to remind him to do it. I wanted to touch his hair myself, to smooth the troubled uncertainty from his brow, but I didn't know how to do it for myself, let alone for him.

"Tommy staying makes sense to me," I insisted. "I can't understand your father not valuing you. I'm so angry that you were hurting and I didn't know, and I still don't know how anyone could be disappointed in you. What you're telling me about your father, I believe you, but it doesn't make sense to me. But how Tommy feels about you makes perfect sense.

"Listen to me, Harvey. You were worried that if I learned more about what was going on with you at home, I might change my mind about you, but I won't. Nothing about your family, and nothing about mine, could make me think less of you. Nothing about your family or mine could make me want to leave you."

I grabbed hold of the sheepskin-lined flaps of his jacket, drawing his ruffled head and his sweet, startled mouth down to mine. I sealed the promise with a kiss.

When I drew back, Harvey's eyes were soft, catching gold light like river water. "Maybe this is why I can't understand Tommy not going. If you asked me to leave Greendale with you," he murmured, "I would go. I'd follow you anywhere."

Warmth bloomed in my chest at his words, then died as the chill of memory went through me. He'd sung a song under my window, garlanded our school with flowers, not for me but because of me. Because I'd cast a spell and made Harvey act like this.

It was your cousin's spell, not yours, the wishing-well spirit's voice whispered in my mind. *His fault, not yours.*

I shouldn't have cast the spell with Ambrose. If I was a witch already, I would have my own grimoire and know the spells in it. If I'd had more power, I could have made sure not to hurt Harvey. If I was stronger than my cousin or the Weird Sisters, I would have cast the right spells.

Power shouldn't only be in the hands of those with cold, fickle hearts. If I wanted better magic, I had to make magic for myself.

I didn't want to give up on being a witch just because some witches were bad. I could be better. I didn't want to give up on power, or making my aunts proud, but I didn't want to give up on Harvey either, and I wasn't going to. I could use magic to protect us both.

Harvey'd been looking at the girl in green, not because she was pretty but because she might take away his adored big brother. He'd been looking at the Weird Sisters and their war-lock boyfriend because he thought they were tourists like the girl in green, people able to easily escape Greendale.

"I'm sorry you were hurt," I told Harvey. "I won't let it happen again. From now on, I'll protect you."

Harvey gave a little laugh, gazing down at me fondly. "I love that you're so fierce. But you can't protect me from everything, 'Brina."

"I can." He didn't have to take the promise seriously. I would. "I will."

I would never let him be hurt again. Harvey might really have cared about me and only me, the way I'd wanted him to, all along. If I'd waited, if I hadn't done the spell with Ambrose, Harvey might have told me that he loved me one day, and I could have believed him.

I would never know now.

It was my own fault. I'd made a terrible mistake.

But I knew how to fix it.

WHAT HAPPENS IN THE DARK

here is a cold spot in Susie Putnam's bedroom where mirrors break.

It is a corner near the window, angled toward the bed. When the mirror isn't there, Susie's walked through it, and the chill there is profound. As if a ghost is leaning close to whisper a secret in Susie's ear, but Susie can't bear the cold long enough to stay and hear.

Susie tries to remember where the place is. Susie can't figure out why it keeps slipping Susie's mind, or where the draft is coming from, whether it is a door or a window or a crack somewhere in the very foundations of Susie's home. Susie's father says he can't even feel the cold. But Susie's sure the chill is not only Susie's imagination. Susie has proof. The corner of Susie's bedroom is the obvious location to position a mirror, so

Susie puts it there, but after a few months, days, or even weeks standing in that corner, a hairline fracture will appear in the glass. Like a crack in ice, barely perceptible at first, then chasing across the mirror's silvery surface and opening to become a dark wound.

For a while, Susie manages to be careful. Susie avoids the corner and keeps the mirror anywhere else.

But sooner or later, something goes wrong.

Sometimes Susie talks with her sad-eyed uncle Jesse, who people say is *sensitive* and *not right* and sometimes even *not a real man*. Or Susie loses her temper and tries to headbutt a sniggering member of the football team, or Susie sleeps and dreams of impossible things. In Susie's dreams, Susie is somewhere different from Greendale. Susie's somewhere glamorous as Susie's misty imaginings of a long-ago past, or Susie's glittering image of a future in which everything has more clarity. In Susie's dreams there are people who understand and sympathize, and when Susie passes Susie hears whispering. They aren't sniggering at Susie the way everybody but Susie's friends do at school. They're calling Susie *handsome*.

"I know you'll be a good girl," Susie's dad says to Susie when he leaves the house. It isn't even a question to him, being good or being a girl, and Susie has to be both. In Susie's father's mind, Susie has no other options. Susie knows he's right.

For whatever reason, Susie can't seem to remember to avoid the cold. Sooner or later, Susie forgets and shoves the mirror into the coldest corner of the bedroom. Sooner or later, Susie wakes from dreams that are too tempting and too horrifying, and has to meet the eyes of the reflection in the bed. Sooner or later, the mirror breaks.

Sometimes, Susie thinks about not avoiding the corner, or throwing away the mirror. Sometimes, Susie thinks about confidently approaching the cracked mirror and looking at it without fearing being swallowed up by the fault into the glass. Seeing what there is to see.

Susie hasn't done it so far.

Sabrina's mortal friends know a lesson Sabrina doesn't, not yet. They have learned to fear themselves. They understand enough to dread the power of a mirror.

WISH GRANTED

The sky curved above me, pearly gray and shimmering and opaque as a clouded mirror. I'd sent Harvey to school ahead of me and walked through the woods on my own, to the lonely riverbank where the spirit of the wishing well waited.

Once I was there, I spilled out every detail of what had happened in the time since I'd last seen her: Ms. Wardwell's bright little cottage, Harvey's hands torn by the thorns, Ambrose being done with me. Then I stopped, almost breathless. I thought she might offer comfort the same way Ms. Wardwell had tried to.

The spirit's silvery eyes were fixed on me, silent and intent. The only thing I could see in them was the reflection of my own desperate face.

"So you want to do the spell now?"

I took a deep breath. "Yes. I want to do the spell now."

The spirit of the wishing well murmured: "That is all you had to say."

It was slightly disconcerting, but I realized she was right. Words didn't mean much. If I intended to be a great witch, I should take action. I found myself nodding.

"I remember the beginning of the spell," I told her. I plunged my hand into that opaque water, up to the wrist, and felt the chill enter my blood. *"Mirror, mirror, make me fairer. Face and heart."*

"Hold your hands out to me," the spirit urged. Embrace the river. Say the words with me.

"Mirror, mirror, make me fairer
Face and heart, all things alter."

I hesitated. "I don't want all things to alter, though."

"Only what you wish," the spirit promised me. "It's your chance."

I reached out to embrace the spirit, and as she receded, my hands found only water. My hands seemed to disappear below the surface, and I thought of Ambrose talking about the story of the girl who would not touch evil and ended up with no hands.

Aunt Hilda had told me that story as well. In the end the girl had new hands made, silver hands. They were better than before. I wanted to be greater, better, the best possible version of myself.

I'd show Ambrose. I'd show them all. When the spirit began to chant, I chanted with her, but I wouldn't say "all things alter." I hummed vague agreement instead, and it seemed to work. Our voices flowed together like two streams joining to form a river.

> *"Mirror, mirror, make me fairer*
> *Face and heart, all things alter*
> *Make me all that I could be*
> *Glory awaits, never falter*
> *Never think to count the cost*
> *Only look into my mirror*
> *Believe there is nothing lost."*

The rustling leaves seemed to repeat the words after us in a hushed refrain. *Lost. Lost. Lost.*

A single ripple, like a shudder, moved across the smooth face of the river. Its silver surface reflected the clouds hanging low over the woods, and the shivering line broke apart the veil. In the mirror of the river, a crack was struck across the sky.

The ripple reached my wrists. The river water suddenly burned, colder than ice.

As water might transform to ice or steam, I felt myself change. This was not the illusion I'd been shown before. My bones felt as if they were being melted down like metal, being reforged into something new. I heard a crackle by my ear, like the sound of fire, and then saw the silvery waterfall on my shoulders. The crackle had been the sound of my own hair, growing years of length in the space of moments. Searing pain shot down the bones of my arms and legs, and I rolled on the dying grass of the riverbank and thrust my feet into the river, feeling the waters cool and soothe the ache. Pain washed down my temples, flaring across the bridge of my nose and shuddering down to my jaw, and I pulled my hands from the river and dropped my face into my wet fingers.

When I lifted my face from my cupped hands, I saw that my fingers had changed, long and slender and finely molded. Even the nails were gleaming, perfect ovals, like cut and polished gemstones.

I leaned over and gazed into the mirror of the waters. My hair was hanging in a sheet of silvery gold around my shoulders. My eyes were wider and clearer, pools of silvery blue. My whole face was formed differently, as though carved afresh in ice, and shining with beauty, as though it might sparkle when the sunlight fell upon it. I looked like a river goddess, a princess born from shimmering sea foam.

I didn't look like myself at all.

"Wait. No," I gasped. "I don't want this. I want to stop."

"Oh, my dear," the spirit murmured, silvery lips laid close

to my ear. Her breath was cold as a wind from the sea. "It's much too late to stop now. Look at yourself."

"It's beautiful, but—"

I tried to pull my feet out of the river. But my legs wouldn't come. There were ties around my ankles, as if my legs had become tangled with waterweeds.

"Would your family know you now?" asked the spirit. "Would that mortal boy you desire see you in a stranger's face? When those that you care for saw you, they saw a collection of features and flaws. Humans always long to be lovely past belief, and never consider that loveliness will be past recognition as well. There is no path back. You can only go forward. With me. Put your hands back in the water."

I hadn't wanted beauty, though. I'd wanted a transformation into greatness, and never even considered that if I transformed, nobody would know me.

I kept staring at the shining girl in the waters. I wouldn't have known myself.

Realization came, sudden and bitter cold. I'd spent so long doubting, but now I was certain again. The spirit's voice was soft but implacable. She hadn't tried to be kind like Ms. Wardwell because she wasn't kind.

I had never seen her come out of the well. She was always lying on the riverbank, waiting for me. She was lying in wait for me. She was *lying*.

"You're not the spirit of the wishing well at all. Are you?"

"No. Can you guess who I am?"

She laughed like silver bells. When she shook her head, her hair flew out into the air like silvery tentacles caught in a current. Aunt Hilda had told me about spirits of wishing wells, but Aunt Zelda had made sure I read books about darker magic. Aunt Zelda had warned me about demons. I remembered those stories now. I remembered illustrations of dangerous creatures, of what darkness might lie beneath the waters, now that I was bound in the river.

"I don't have to guess," I whispered. "I know who you are now. You are a creature like Melusine, the demon serpent of the river who killed with her kiss. You are the mirror of a dead witch queen. You are a rusalka who waits on the riverbanks, combs your hair and sings, lures your victims into the river and then tangles their feet with the weeds that are your hair."

"I always sing the same song," the rusalka mused. "Come to me, my darling, you are special, you are chosen, you are unique, just like everybody else. It worked on you, didn't it? It works every time."

"And you plan to drown me," I stated. "Just like everybody else."

The spirit, hovering at my shoulder, drew a finger cold as an icicle down my cheek. "Well. Perhaps you are a little more special than some of the others."

"Fool me once, shame on you. Fool me twice, I get drowned. I'm not falling for that again."

"The last girl had golden hair and a green coat," the spirit said dreamily. "I showed the illusion in the river, of her face made perfect, surrounded by city and marquee lights. She reached her hands out eagerly for death, and I drowned her. That's how it is with most victims. A small, simple thing. Why waste any more magic on them than that? They do it to themselves, really. They throw themselves at me. All I have to do is catch them and drag them down. But you *are* different. I poured magic into you. I poured myself into you."

Golden hair and a green coat and marquee lights, I thought with a shudder. Tommy's girlfriend Alison, who had gone away so suddenly to LA. She hadn't made it out of Greendale after all.

"Am I different in a way where I can persuade you to let me go?"

"Oh no," said the rusalka. "I don't let victims go. I drown them all. But I drown some differently than others. Mortals say witches cannot drown because witches can make bargains with the elements. You're a witch, and I'm going to give you a choice. What do you think that choice might be?"

I didn't have to think about it. I'd already seen my new glimmering reflection. She'd already told me what she wanted.

"You pour yourself into me."

"Exactly," the rusalka agreed in her silky, silvery whisper. "You the vessel, and I the shining water within. All of your dreams can come true after all, for the low price of working with me. You walk out of this clearing with my river rushing through your bloodstream. You cannot go home, but there is still a place for a magical girl, and you know where that place is. You and I will go to the Academy of Unseen Arts together, and everyone will be dazzled by this strange witch, irresistible in her beauty and power.

"Say yes. The other choice is drowning now. My water-weeds are stronger than chains. You can't escape them."

I'd be in chains either way. I was very certain about how little control I would have with this spirit piloting my body like a boat upon her waters. If I let this demonic spirit possess me, my family would never know what had happened to me. They would think I was dead. It might as well be true.

I stopped struggling and kicking. I tested the hold of the water, as a mortal prisoner might test the strength of the knots they were tied with and find give in a rope. The waters were cold as chains, but I felt them shiver as I moved.

I was stronger than she thought. I could still get out.

I tensed all my muscles and my magic for the burst of effort needed to escape. Just before I moved, I remembered Tommy's girlfriend Alison waiting by her car at the edge of the woods, and what Ms. Wardwell had said to me.

I have found several young people rambling by that river near dark … I can't think why that spot draws them so. I remembered my teacher's worried face, behind her big spectacles, and the warm refuge of her little house. I wished I were there now.

I wondered how many people Ms. Wardwell had saved from the river, without even knowing she was saving them.

I wondered how many people she'd failed to save. Nobody knew the mortals were in danger, and when they disappeared, nobody ever knew what became of them.

Until me. I knew.

The rusalka was luring mortals to her river to drown them. She would lure more if nobody stopped her, and I could imagine who those mortals might be.

The memories crowded down upon me, thick as the fall of leaves when summer died. Roz's eyes going unfocused as she looked at herself in the mirror. Susie, studiously avoiding her own reflection as if it were a stranger she did not want to meet. My Harvey, who had been terrified in the Hall of Mirrors as a child, who thought he was disappointing his father simply by being who he was. Any one of them might leap for the chance to be transformed.

When I remembered how Ms. Wardwell talked about finding other kids wandering by the side of this river, when I imagined the rusalka's future prey, I saw the mortal faces I loved.

One mortal I loved had been hurt already, because of me.

I'd promised him today: never again. I wasn't going to run away to keep myself safe and leave my mortal friends in danger.

The rusalka's voice was sweet as a song. "What do you say? Do you agree?"

"I agree," I said. My own voice was starting to sound more like hers. The chime of silver bells was in it, faint but growing nearer. "On one condition. I want to go home first. I want to go stand outside my childhood home, so I can say goodbye to my childhood."

She seemed amused by the request.

"Agreed. Now under the water with you, and breathe me in. You need water for a rebirth as well as a death."

She slipped from my side into the water without a splash.

I felt the pull of the waterweeds, strangling tight around my legs, dragging me down. The earth beneath me was turning to mud as I slid inexorably into the water. I only had a moment.

"No fire, no sun, no moon shall burn me
No water, no loch, no sea shall drown me."

My fingers traced patterns on the air, and then I was pulled down under the water. I thought the icy cold might stop my heart.

When my feet hit the riverbed, bones crunched beneath

234

my shoes. My eyes flew open, and I saw the truth of the river in the murk beneath the gleaming waters.

The riverbed was white with a thick blanket of bones. Bones had buried any river stones, but among the grinning skulls and shattered tibiae there were different fragments of mortality: the billow of a ragged green coat, the sorrowful shine of a tiny diamond ring, a shoe with its laces untied and waving forlornly in the dark currents.

I drifted, drowning in horror. It was a shock when the leering face, transparent as sea foam, came at me with its mouth open and serrated teeth glittering in its maw. A scream escaped my lips, a silent silver bubble that would break on the surface and never reach human ears.

Suddenly my body propelled itself through the water, sleek as a seal. I didn't make the decision to scramble out, but I was climbing from the river. I was on the riverbank, but I wasn't the one pulling myself out.

I have not forgotten our agreement. The rusalka's voice echoed against the confines of my skull. *A sad goodbye to your childhood home. Then I take full possession, and we go.*

No water shall drown me. I'd said the words. I had to trust in my spell, but it was hard to do as I felt an icy fist clenching around my heart, cold wrapping my bones, the river rushing through my veins. My red dress, soaked by river water, clung to me as if I were dipped in blood.

"I can't say you didn't warn me. You drown them all," I said. "You'll drown me in the sea chambers of my own heart, under the sound of wind and water. Until I'm drowned out."

Her laugh was a chill in my blood.

In the very deeps, I might hear you scream sometimes.

My new, longer legs ate up the forest floor, taking me near the curve of the path so I could peer at what lay beyond the trees.

The cemetery behind the ringed fence, the tall house with its towering chimneys, sharply peaked roof, and witches inside. I clung to a branch, and squinted through the trees, and stared. Home. I wanted so badly to be safe at home.

Time to go, whispered the rusalka inside my mind.

"Yeah," I whispered back. "Time to go."

My eyes stung from peering. Tears fell, impossibly cold when they had always been warm before. Then I loosed my hold on the branch and hurled myself, not into the woods but away from them.

I raced wildly down the path, running desperately for home. I knew it might be hopeless. Why would they take a stranger in?

WHAT HAPPENS IN THE DARK

A mbrose used to sit on the roof and feed the birds. The treetops whispered the news to the clouds and the flocks as they went by: A witch who is grounded wants to be with creatures that fly. Witches don't tend to attract doves or bluebirds. Instead there were buzzards, and even a vulture that circled around Ambrose as he walked over the sloping rooftops, hovering around his head as he stood on the edge.

It wasn't like having a familiar or freedom again, but it was what he had.

"Get rid of that vulture," Auntie Z. ordered when Sabrina came. "Think of the baby."

"Make up with Sabrina," Auntie Z. told him this morning, when he wouldn't come down to breakfast. "You're older and you should know better."

"And yet," said Ambrose, "I never do. Sabrina can stop being such a total raving witch."

He stayed in his room, sprawled on his bed under his draped curtains and chiaroscuro drawings, and indulged in a sulk.

What Sabrina doesn't consider is the fact they weren't Ambrose's first family. Or even his second. First was the family he was born into, the father who died so young that Ambrose will never have a chance to stop being childish, wanting his father's approval or fearing his disapproval. His father's disappointment in Ambrose is an eternal fact graven in stone, a sentence passed that cannot be erased, and all Ambrose has ever done is live up to that.

Hilda cared for him when his father was gone. With sweet Hilda came stern Zelda, the two so inextricably linked they never seem far apart, sleeping in twin beds even with an ocean between them. Auntie Hilda wrapped Ambrose up in love, spoiled him, never said no to him.

But Ambrose always wanted more, and more. It's how he got less.

That was how his second family came to pass. He went searching for a father figure and found a leader, found brothers-in-arms, and it was no real surprise when his co-conspirators led him into actual crime. He didn't question their ideals, or the fiery end result. When it all went wrong he thought of blazing defiance, and a martyr's death.

His nature has always been explosive.

He never considered imprisonment that would last this long. If he were a mortal, he would have died in this house already. Sometimes he thinks his sentence was genius: that they knew the one punishment Ambrose could not bear was dreariness. Tomorrow and tomorrow and tomorrow creep before him, within the walls of the house, within the confines of these grounds. He will be held corralled in this small space until his soul dwindles within him, and all his fire goes out.

Edward Spellman was always going places, and Ambrose was always staying right where he was. Sabrina's father never thought much of him, or he would've tried to help Ambrose. So Ambrose never thought much about Edward, other than the interest anyone would take in a man with that meteoric a rise and fall. Becoming High Priest, changing the laws of the witching world, marrying a mortal, living and dying on an epic scale Ambrose couldn't achieve. If Edward had survived, Ambrose imagines he wouldn't have wanted his daughter to associate with Ambrose much.

Ambrose never planned to have anything to do with her. Sabrina was a baby who arrived in the Spellman residence and took up too much of Auntie Hilda's attention. She woke up screaming at all hours of the night, and he could not leave the house or escape from her. But he was bored, so he'd play with her, partly to amuse her, and partly to amuse himself. Sabrina had a solemn face—she still does—but he could always get her to smile for him.

I'm nothing but a toy to you, Sabrina said. Maybe she's right. Maybe she's smart, and maybe now she's realized what both their fathers knew: that all Ambrose will ever be is a disappointment.

She was sweet, but Ambrose doesn't find babies that interesting. It wasn't then that she got him. It was later. Sabrina as a little girl in a smock dress and buckled shoes. Even then, she wore a perpetual tiny frown, already feeling responsible for the world. When they were done playing, she would conscientiously tidy away her toys into their correct places, while Ambrose left the toys scattered across the floor until somebody tripped over them.

He'd do magic for her, because it made her laugh and look at him as if he was a marvel, and Ambrose is susceptible to flattery.

Once he made her rocking horse take off on a wild gallop around the room, and Sabrina fell and smacked her little face right into the wall.

Sabrina burst into tears, and Ambrose went from a lounge to an alarmed crouch, about to call out for Auntie Hilda or Auntie Z., when Sabrina came running into his arms. She was crying as though her little heart would break, tears and snot on his dressing gown, small hands locked determinedly about his neck. Even as he patted her back and rocked her, he was looking around for the person she *should* have run to, someone who would never have hurt her in the first place. Someone she could depend on.

"Sabrina, Sabrina," he said helplessly into her golden hair. "You're making a mistake. You've got the wrong guy."

He was setting up a fun spell in the attic a few days later, and he heard Auntie Hilda cry out: "Sabrina!" He found himself halfway down the stairs, heart hammering in his ears and spell ingredients abandoned far behind him, before he could even think. It was an unfamiliar feeling, being afraid and angry at the thought that anything might dare touch a hair on her golden head.

He found himself calling her *cousin* as if that would give him a better claim on her, a right to be part of her life when he wasn't supposed to be. He stopped spending so much time on the roof, and the birds found somewhere else to fly.

Auntie Hilda suggested they send Sabrina to the mortal school in Greendale—because Sabrina was half mortal, because her mother, Diana, would have wanted that for her. Ambrose thinks Sabrina's mother must have been remarkable, not because Edward loved her, but because Hilda loved her enough to respect Diana's wishes for her daughter just as much as Edward's. Auntie Z. was against it: What could Sabrina learn in a mundane school? They didn't even teach Latin, and unless you learned Latin at age five, you were never going to be truly fluent.

Ambrose surprised his aunts and himself by entering the battle on Auntie Hilda's side and emerging victorious. He didn't want Sabrina to be trapped in this house too.

When Sabrina went to school, he missed her more than he'd expected. He spent a long day in the attic on her first day of school, listening for the sound of those buckle shoes running up the curving lane, past the burial ground and the twisted tree and their yellow sign, up the steps of their house and back to him.

When she got home, Sabrina sat with him and poured out her stories about her friends, brand-new but already beloved: Harvey, Roz, Susie, and Harvey again.

Harvey, Harvey, always Harvey. Sabrina is a girl with a lot of decision, and she believes her decisions are right. Ambrose always aspired to and could never reach the certainty Sabrina was born with. She's her father's daughter, as he couldn't manage to be his father's son. She's one of life's fixers, in a broken world. She looks on tempests and is never shaken.

Ambrose is a tempest, confined to a teapot. He isn't ever going to be able to change Sabrina's mind or her heart when she has that mind or heart set on something.

If she set her mind on helping him, he almost believes she could do it, but she's always worried about her friends. She's never known Ambrose as anything but a prisoner in his own home. Worrying about him never seems to occur to her, and sometimes he hates her for that.

But is he worth her concern?

He fought for her to leave the house and go to school, and then he was jealous of her for escaping when he couldn't. If he were a better man, he wouldn't resent her. If he were as wise and magical and experienced as he pretends for her, he wouldn't make the mistakes he does. She's starting to catch on to what he knew all along. Ambrose can't be trusted.

He never would have cared about the details of a mortal life if he hadn't been trapped here. He shows off for her, but it might be for his own vanity.

This is his third family, and third time's supposed to be the charm. Witches, especially Ambrose, believe in charm. But sometimes charm is empty. Sometimes charm is not enough. Surely a family should be something better than broken pieces almost forced together, trying to form a whole.

Ambrose used to think he should have a real family. He knows Sabrina should.

Long ago Ambrose got used to hearing a pair of sneakers, shuffling in the dust beside the decided tap of Sabrina's buckled shoes. Harvey walked Sabrina home for years before they were sweethearts, the faithful suitor. Occasionally these days Sabrina even lets Harvey come inside and say hello to her aunts or to Ambrose.

Once Sabrina and Harvey were talking to Auntie Hilda in the kitchen, and Ambrose was looking out the windows as he often does. He saw another boy waiting for Harvey outside: a few years older than Harvey, with brown curling hair a shade away from Harvey's. Tommy, the big brother Harvey talked so often and worshipfully about.

Honestly, Ambrose only gave him a second look because he was cute: football player shoulders, big blue eyes, a cross shining against his flannel shirt. More Ambrose's type than Harvey, though they both had the same air of being too well-behaved to bother with. But then the door of the Spellman house opened, and Harvey came out.

Tommy's eyes lit up, and he reached out as if it was easy, and Harvey leaned against him as if it was natural. The two brothers walked away down the road together, with Harvey tucked under the protective curve of Tommy's arm. Harvey touched his brother in the same way Tommy wore his cross, with almost absentminded faith in something that would always be there and always be bigger than himself. The ideal big brother, someone you could rely on, someone who gave without grudging. Someone solid and dependable, not wild and wildly vacillating.

Ambrose couldn't shake the thought: That's the kind of person Sabrina deserves to have by her side. That's probably the kind of person Sabrina *wants* on her side.

Ambrose could never be that.

Now he tosses restlessly on his bed with the darkness closing in, only a roof between him and the sky, so close but so far from freedom.

She was born for great things, born to fly. She was always going to be gone like his father, like his familiar, like his friends, like the birds. He was always going to let her down. Why not now, rather than later?

He's been listening for her step for years: along the curving lane, past the tree and the burial ground. He knows the sound by heart. He hears her step now, running too fast, almost stumbling. Through the night, and back to him.

Sabrina, in trouble.

It wouldn't matter if it were the whole coven, or the hounds of hell, or Satan himself after her.

Ambrose never really thought he could feel responsible for anybody.

THE CRUCIBLE

I tore down the path, past the cemetery with its heap of fresh earth. Dust rose in puffs beneath my heels, as if the earth was panting with me. Like a river to the ocean, I went home.

The rusalka's voice shrieked through my blood as she realized she didn't have as firm a grip on me as she'd believed. *What are you doing? Stop!*

Nothing could have made me stop. I was running for my life.

I could see my front door. I was almost at my porch steps, with its toad statues standing guard.

A ribbon of cold shot down my arm. For a moment it seemed like a silver vein had sprung right out of my wrist. The jet of silver water leaped for the porch steps and, fast as a tidal wave, a great gleaming silver spiderweb barred my way. I didn't stop running. I couldn't let myself stop. If I did, I was lost.

Behind the silver veil, my front door slammed open with shattering force. Blurred as if there was a mirror between us, I glimpsed a swirl of red velvet robes, and I heard the roar of a spell. A jagged tear slashed through the spiderweb as though it had been cut with a knife.

I didn't check my stride. I burst through the remnants of silver threads and spells, flew up my porch steps, and found safe landing in my cousin's arms. I was too tall now, we were horribly the same height, but I flung a desperate arm around his neck, grabbed his red velvet dressing gown in my fist, and put my head down on his shoulder.

"Please, Ambrose," I sobbed. "Please help me, please know me. I'm Sabrina."

"I know that," Ambrose said into my hair, his voice shockingly calm. "I've spent years listening for your step coming down the road to our house. What is that *thing*?"

His arm locked around my waist, possessive and protective, holding me close. I swallowed a last sob against the velvet and turned in the circle of his arm. "It's a river demon. I met it the day I went to find the forget-me-not for our spell, and she pretended to be a wishing-well spirit, and I made a wish."

248

"She's possessing you?" he demanded.

"Not yet. I cast a spell, to make sure she couldn't drown me, but she—she did this to me, and she's killing mortals—she'll kill more—"

"No, she won't." Ambrose's jaw was set.

The fluttering, hanging shreds of the spiderweb had come alive, tiny silver threads joining back up, forming a silvery mass that would take a new shape. My cousin and I stood together on our porch, facing down whatever the creature might become.

A voice rang through our open door.

"Ambrose, *must* you embrace random floozies on our porch?" Aunt Zelda asked with some annoyance.

My aunt strolled out, an impeccable vision in teal wool, elaborate lace, and high heels, apparently too focused on floozies to notice the spells and spiderwebs and tears.

"Yes, I must!" declared Ambrose. "It is my right! But as it happens, this particular floozy is Sabrina."

Aunt Zelda squinted at me. Her eyes traveled from my face to my hairband.

"So it is. Forgive me, darling. What ghastly thing has happened to you?"

Ambrose answered for me. "She went into the woods to find spell ingredients for me, stumbled upon what she thought was a wishing-well spirit, made a wish, and got spanked by the Monkey's Paw."

Aunt Zelda made a disapproving noise. "So this is your fault."

"Yes," said Ambrose.

"No," I said, at the same time. "It's all my fault. But—*watch out*!" The river spirit seethed and took on a twisted new form, half silver panther, half engulfing storm, leaping for us.

"How dare you? This is Spellman ground!" Aunt Zelda snapped out a spell.

The rusalka shuddered, shredding from the bottom up, its ragged tentacles writhing. I screamed. Pain cut me off at the knees, but Ambrose's arm was an iron bar. He was holding me up. He wouldn't let me fall.

She said my words. She's bound to me, said the spirit. *Give her to me, or kill her with your spells.*

All my life, I'd told myself magic could fix anything.

Ambrose made a face. "Magic won't work. We can't banish it without banishing Sabrina with it, unless it's defeated first. Hey, river demon! I challenge you to a game of Scrabble."

His voice was light and playful, but I could feel the tensed strength of the arm holding me, and hear the furious hammer of his heart.

"Better hope the demon doesn't notice you cheat to get the

triple word score," I muttered, and Ambrose laughed, and I truly understood for the first time how my cousin lived his life, with laughter a shield against pain and fear.

"How do we fight without magic?" Aunt Zelda demanded.

"How do witch-hunters fight magic?" Ambrose asked. "With their blades and guns."

Through the fading agony I heard Aunt Zelda say the very alarming words: "Tell me if this hurts, darling."

She produced her glittering cigarette holder from the lapel of her woolen jacket, then viciously stabbed the river demon with its tiny pointed pitchfork ends. I heard the rusalka scream like the sound of water whipped by a gale.

"No!" I called out between my teeth. "It doesn't hurt."

"My thanks to our merciless Dark Lord." Aunt Zelda nodded. "Ambrose, do you happen to have a sword?"

"Gosh," remarked Ambrose. "I think I left my sword in the pocket of my other dressing gown."

It seemed unlikely that Aunt Zelda could vanquish a river demon with her cigarette holder, though if anyone could, it would be her. I looked around for a weapon and saw Ambrose and Aunt Zelda scan our surroundings as well. I didn't know if there was time for one of us to run inside and seize anything, but we had to try. I unclenched my fingers from where they were twisted in Ambrose's dressing gown.

"Let go of me," I whispered.

"I'm not planning to do that, Sabrina," Ambrose replied steadily.

The rusalka was gathering itself for another leap: not to attack my aunt or my cousin this time, I thought. The shimmering mercury of her body was forming another shape, a tall girl with long hair. She was coming for me, to take possession.

Aunt Zelda stepped out in front of me. Ambrose turned, setting his shoulder against mine, making his body a shield for mine.

The spirit collapsed into a puddle of silver, dwindling down to reveal Aunt Hilda, her hair and dress streaked with grave dirt. She lowered the shovel she was holding.

"Lucky you killed me earlier, Zelda," she said breathlessly. "I always wish that you wouldn't leave the shovel you bury me with lying around, but I suppose that came in handy too. Sabrina, my love! What did that creature do to your pretty face?"

"Quick, we have to stop it," I said.

I threaded my fingers through Ambrose's and pulled him down the porch steps, past our small guardian toad statues to circle the quicksilver pool and stand with Aunt Hilda. She held my hand too. Aunt Hilda reached out her muddy hand for Aunt Zelda's, and Aunt Zelda clasped it and Ambrose's free hand.

"You didn't make a real bargain with me, demon," I said. "And I didn't make one with you. I didn't say 'all things alter,' because I never wanted to alter everything about myself. I love myself too much for that."

"Love . . ." The pool became a wisp of a girl, almost a wraith. She was laughing. "If you love yourself so much, let me make a new bargain with you. Pick yourself out, and I'll let you keep yourself. Pick the wrong one, and I'll keep you instead."

My aunts and Ambrose began to protest. I shouted them down. "Deal."

Silver water sketched images against the sky, more beautiful than Harvey's drawings. One showed a witch queen on a throne, one showed a girl in her lover's embrace. One showed a little girl, with her mom and her dad holding both her hands. One showed a girl with her aunts and her cousin, laughing and carefree, another a girl with her friends whispering secrets.

"Which one is you?" the river demon asked. "*Which one?*"

I looked at all those lovely princesses in the air. I wanted to reach out and grab each perfect image.

Instead I drew mine and Ambrose's linked hands to my breast. I pointed to my own flawed and wildly beating heart.

"This one," I said.

The silver images dissolved. All that was left was the pool at our feet. My legs were too long, my face felt wrong, but all trace of her was gone from my veins. She couldn't hurt me now.

We stood linked in a circle around our enemy.

The Spellman witches, on Spellman ground.

"You do the honors, Sabrina," suggested Aunt Zelda.

Ambrose whispered the words in my ear. I stepped forward, just one step, so our circle remained unbroken, and called out the words of the spell to the sky.

> *"Earth and air, fire and water*
> *I am your daughter.*
> *Punish my foes for their sins*
> *Let them be torn by all four winds,*
> *Be buried, be burned, and then,*
> *Never to come back again."*

The rusalka gave a high, thin whine, the sound of water in a kettle about to boil. The silvery pool began to evaporate off our ground, rising in a thick gray wisp, denser than steam. It was like the smoke coiling from the flame of a single great candle.

"Go on, love," whispered Aunt Hilda. "It's almost your birthday, after all."

I drew in my breath, hesitated, and blew what remained of the river demon away. To all four winds.

We watched the smoke dissipate and almost disintegrate, and the last gray grains floated over the treetops, away from our woods and far, far away from our house.

"That's that," said Aunt Zelda, tucking her cigarette holder away. "We will shortly be having serious words about river demons, Sabrina, but for now let me assemble what we will need to take that horrid demon's spell off you and get you back to normal."

Aunt Hilda grimaced. "I need to wash up. Awful how grave dirt gets in your ears."

Aunt Hilda climbed the porch steps, Aunt Zelda following her.

"Wait, wait, aunties," Ambrose called out. "Let's not be hasty. The new nose is great. Cousin, do you want to consider keeping the nose?"

He pretended to catch my nose between his fingers.

I laughed, shaking my head. "I like my own nose."

"Yes, I suppose I do too," Ambrose allowed.

The front door closed behind my aunts, leaving my cousin and me standing outside in front of our house alone together. I'd run to him and clung to him and fought by his side, and for that whole stretch of time I'd forgotten our bitter quarrel. I remembered now.

I looked at the ground where the rusalka had stood, before

it went up in smoke. "Thank you. I know you must be angry with me after last night, so—thanks."

"You imagined that I'd leave you possessed by a river demon because we had a little tiff?" Ambrose asked mildly. "Seems an overreaction."

I lifted my chin, and met his eyes. They were not rolling white with outrage as they had been last night, or dark with protective fury. His gaze now felt like a question.

So I answered him. "No, I didn't think that for a minute. I've been having all kinds of stupid doubts, but when I was terrified in the woods, I knew that if I could get home to you, I'd be safe. I realize this is prison to you, but it's home to me, because this is where you and my aunts are. I got mad because I wish it was home for you too, but I'll try to understand how you feel more. I can't imagine what it's like to be trapped in a prison."

I wasn't sure what else to say, and I could hear Aunt Zelda calling for me. So I nodded awkwardly to my cousin, and climbed up the porch steps leading to home.

Ambrose's thoughtful voice caught me and held me still on the steps. "Can you imagine what it's like to be in a prison, shut up in the dark, and to find a window? Only a small window, but the light shines through."

I shook my head, frowning. I wasn't sure what he was getting at.

Ambrose looked up to where I stood, and then walked up the steps to join me, his red dressing gown flaring behind him with every dramatic stride. My merry, mischievous cousin's face was serious. He paused briefly on the step beside me, and spoke with his eyes on the front door, without glancing in my direction.

"You aren't nothing to me. You're not a toy. But I got used to thinking of you as a child. I wanted to indulge you, but I should have wanted you to understand. I'm sorry for that."

He started up the steps as soon as he said it, so I couldn't answer him. I could only hurry after him.

Before we went inside the house, my cousin stopped once more. He reached out, unusually for him, and with one light finger against my jaw he tilted my chin, and looked into my strange new face as though he would always know exactly who I was.

"You are sunlight in prison to me," said Ambrose. "Harvey's spell is not what you think."

WHAT HAPPENS IN THE DARK

S tone walls echo with a witch's song.
　　Father Blackwood, High Priest of the Church of Night, Faustus to his intimates, nods along as the orphan witch Prudence practices for the infernal choir.

> "When Satan comes with thunder and lamentation
> And drowns the world in blood, what joy shall fill my
> 　heart!
> Then I shall bow in proud adoration
> And proclaim Dark Lord how great thou art!"

Father Blackwood applauds. "Excellent, Prudence, excellent."

In the stone chamber, among lightless candles, Prudence's unusually lovely face glows with hope. "Thank you, Father.

Do you think—do you think Lady Blackwood will like this song?"

"I am certain she will," Father Blackwood lies. "And even if she doesn't, you'll keep trying, won't you?"

Prudence nods. "Of course, Father Blackwood."

Father Blackwood winks at her, and pats her arm. As he does so, he notices his fingernails could do with some sharpening. It is important to take pride in yourself. "I knew you would."

He strides away down the stone passageways of the Academy of Unseen Arts, as Prudence gazes after him with what he recognizes as awe. Most of his students regard him that way.

Prudence looks up to him as all the students do, as though he were their father. Of course, Prudence actually *is* his daughter, but that doesn't matter. It's not as if she was his son, or her mother his wife. Prudence's mother was a weak woman, and the child she left behind is the same. Prudence doesn't know, and it is better for her not to know.

Far better to have Prudence ignorant of the truth, scrambling for approval rather than expecting affection. Far better to have his wife, Constance, fear that truth, and hate Prudence for it rather than him. Prudence's songs will always sound like fear and funeral bells to Constance, no matter if Prudence sings until her throat bleeds trying to please her.

The whole situation is ideal. The book *The Witch's Hammer* is right about some things: It is dangerous when a woman thinks alone. Once you fill a woman full of doubts, she can be made useful.

Certainty is the property of men. Father Blackwood is certain of this.

Still, he considers Prudence one of the best students in the Academy. Among the witches, who will naturally always be worth less than the warlocks. Prudence is beautiful, cruel, proud, and powerful. Blackwood supposes that it must be his blood coming out in her. Blackwood likes a woman with spirit, if that spirit can be broken by him.

He stops by another student as he does his rounds, studying among the restricted books, and says indulgently: "Ah, Nicholas. Working hard?"

Nick has a cubbyhole set up with black candles and piles of books that the other students don't dare touch. There is a calendar set up there now, with inky crosses marking the days until Halloween. Nick Scratch is a promising pupil, Father Blackwood considers, but his greatest flaw is that he is perhaps a little too intelligent. The boy is always studying Edward Spellman's old books, or wandering the earth like the warlock Cain once had. Books and travel lead to questions, and that can lead to questioning orders.

Nick ignores him, dark head bent over his book. Father Blackwood looks over Nicholas's shoulder and spies the words *All days are nights to see till I see thee.*

"Nicholas," he says in tones of horrified dismay, "is this *love poetry?*"

"It's Shakespeare," Nick says curtly.

"Good name, but I don't think I know—" Father Blackwood stops, stricken by a terrible thought. "Are you reading a book written by a *mortal?* About—about—I can't even say it. How dare you bring filth like that into my school! What if one of the younger children, Satan forbid, got hold of this?"

He snaps his fingers. The book in Nick's hands bursts into soothing orange and purple flame, seething over white page and black words. A scarlet tongue of fire licks across Nick's palm.

Nick erupts from his chair. Father Blackwood isn't fool enough to think that Nick is reacting because of something as ultimately meaningless as physical suffering. Nicholas is not one of the weak pupils who died begging for absurd things like pity or making the pain stop. Soft souls are crushed by the weight of the Academy.

Nick's face is set, hard as the stone of their Dark Lord's statue. In the iris of one dark eye, there is a flicker of flame that burns deeper crimson than blood, a reflection of hellfire.

Oh, Father Blackwood *does* love some truly sinful wrath. Nick is a *very* promising pupil.

After a simmering moment, Father Blackwood relents. "That's done with, and we'll say no more about it. No more reading trash, eh? Read something educational, about magic and murder. That's a bad boy. Or go talk sense with your fellow warlocks. You spend altogether too much time surrounded by witches. I understand the lure of saucy, curvaceous flesh as well as the next warlock, but life can't be all wicked carnality, can it?"

"No," says Nick.

Encouraged by this sign of submission, Father Blackwood slaps the boy on the back. "More's the pity."

He turns away with a flick of his robes, putting all his promising and unpromising pupils firmly behind him as he stalks through the halls of ghosts and magic and monuments to evil that he rules, making his way to his private chambers.

Once within his inner unsanctified sanctum, his nostrils flare and he swings around in a wary circle. For a moment everything seems as usual: red velvet curtains, black-shaded lamps, shelves of grimoires, a tasteful crocodile hanging from the ceiling, a fire almost leaping from the confines of a tall, narrow grate. Then his eye catches the streamers of orange flame, reflected in a silvery surface.

Before his roaring fire cowers a much reduced river demon. She is a sorry sight, like a broken silver reed.

"And what do *you* have to say for yourself?" Father Blackwood demands.

She shrinks before him, but that does not appease his wrath at all.

"You had one job! To corrupt and possess! That is the whole

point of demons. The Dark Lord's signs and portents have been very clear." Father Blackwood sighs. "That half-mortal girl is important. I might have had her completely in my power, and used her to achieve glory for the loyal warlocks of the Church of Night. Except that you catastrophically failed to take Sabrina, and destroyed all my schemes."

"I beg your forgiveness," the river demon babbles. "I throw myself at your feet."

"What good does that do me? The Dark Lord may even send someone else into what should be my domain, to make certain that he will secure Sabrina. The prospect is appalling." Father Blackwood shudders.

He doesn't much care for the idea of an important girl. He'd relished the idea of this witch with her sullied blood coming to the Academy already his creature, a beautiful evil handmaiden with no will of her own. He'd imagined a ready-made tool in his hands. Now she would come on Halloween, and who knew what ideas she might have in her head, and what trouble she would cause?

Fortunately, there is the possibility of other schemes. He is an expert schemer.

"All is not lost, however," Faustus Blackwood muses. "There is still Zelda Spellman, who admires me so much. A clever woman, but like all women, in need of the guidance of men. She is faithful in her attendance to the Church of Night, and she is clearly worried about her wayward niece with impure blood, as well she might be. Zelda is a devoted servant of Satan, and respects me highly. By far the best approach would be to drop a hint in Zelda's ear that the head of the Church of Night is standing by, ready to help her with her family troubles. I imagine she will weep with gratitude, kiss my feet, and deliver her niece to me on a silver platter with a delicious garnish."

He nods to himself with satisfaction.

"The cousin, Ambrose Spellman, may prove helpful as well," he decides. "Really, the punishment for his youthful indiscretion has gone on long enough. What adventurous warlock hasn't at least considered blowing up various holy locations? Ambrose showed commendable loyalty to his co-conspirators by not turning them in, and I see a clear path to winning that loyalty for my own. I'm sure he's frantic to escape from that house of women. Desperation is very motivating. He would be deeply grateful, I imagine, to the benefactor who granted him freedom. Oh yes, all is far from lost. Coercion, seduction, bribery… the possibilities for the Spellman family are endless."

He rubs his hands together, his ruby ring catching the light.

"Who shall I seduce?" asks the rusalka.

"Nobody asked you to seduce anybody!" Blackwood snaps. "I planned to be the one doing the seducing. Do you doubt my powers of seduction?"

"Not at all, my master!" the rusalka says hastily. "I'm certain you can be very seductive. Who are you planning to seduce?"

"Whoever seems the most useful."

Zelda, for preference. Father Blackwood has grievous doubts about Hilda. Once he'd asked her what her thoughts were on unbridled carnality, and Hilda answered that she wasn't fond of riding horses. What kind of witch preferred making jam to making love? It was hardly decent.

"Yes, master," whispers the spirit. "How may I aid you in your schemes?"

Father Blackwood raises an eyebrow. "You? Oh, I'm afraid that you are no longer of any use to me at all."

She doesn't even have a chance to whimper before he seizes her by the throat, whispering black magic into her ear as she shrieks and struggles. Pain turns to agony, screams for mercy turn into screams for an end, and eventually the river demon is nothing but a silvery smear on the heel of his supple black leather boot.

When Sabrina comes to the Academy of Unseen Arts, Faustus Blackwood intends to crush her beneath his heel as well. The half witch has no idea what is waiting for her, come Halloween.

STARTING THE FALL

I asked Harvey to meet me in the woods early the next morning, telling him I had a confession to make. I got up before sunrise, and from my bedroom window I watched sky and treetops change from gray to green to pure gold. I fixed a black hairband in my short blond hair, slid on a fuzzy black-and-white cardigan, put on my red coat, and left home whistling.

At the edge of our property waited a tall witch, leaning against a tree and wearing zipped-up athletic clothes rather than her usual prim dark dress. Even more unusual, she was alone.

"You're looking pleased with yourself," Prudence remarked sourly. "So I suppose whatever was bothering you is resolved. I thought you might really be in trouble this time. Everything comes so easily to you, doesn't it, Sabrina?"

"I wouldn't say that. And as fellow witches, shouldn't we refrain from flinging accusations at each other? No need to be all *I saw Goody Proctor with the Devil.*"

"What?" said Prudence. "Who are you saying had the great honor of being with the Dark Lord?"

I sighed. "Never mind. I'm not in any trouble. Thanks for your concern."

Prudence gave a jeering laugh. "That's a pity. I'd hoped something would stop you from entering the Academy of Unseen Arts, but I see I'll just have to beat you—in every possible meaning of the word—once you're there."

She tossed her arrogant head. It was odd to see Prudence without her sisters, and less perfectly turned out than normal. She'd come here early, by herself. Maybe, I thought for the strangest moment, she actually had felt something like concern.

I reached out and laid my hand on Prudence's arm. "It doesn't have to be a competition, you know."

Prudence shoved my hand away. "Everything has to be a competition. So I can win."

Well, I'd tried. I sighed, and shrugged, and left Prudence standing alone under the tree.

I made my way into the depths of the forest, to the place where Harvey had asked to meet.

He'd asked, "Do you remember the wishing well we found last year?" and been confused when I had to laugh. He was waiting for me in the clearing where I had gone yesterday to make a bargain.

Harvey was not near the silver ribbon of the silent river. He was standing near the well. His hands were in his pockets, his head slightly bowed and his shoulders curved slightly inward. When he heard me, his chin lifted and his spine straightened. Even though I'd arranged to meet him here, he smiled as if I was a wonderful surprise.

I wondered for a moment what Harvey would have thought if he'd seen me the way I was yesterday.

I didn't think he would have looked at me like this, and I never wanted him to look at me any other way.

"'Brina." Harvey smiled and reached out a hand for mine.

I didn't take it. I stared down at the tall grass and loose stones around the well instead. If I looked at him for too long, if I thought about how much I didn't want to lose him, I might not say what I had to say.

"Let me get this out right away, before I lose my nerve. I had no idea that the girl in green was Tommy's girlfriend," I burst out. "I didn't know anything was bothering you. I *did* think you were looking at her because she was beautiful and glamorous. And the next day, I thought you were looking at that group of witches because they were all pretty."

"Um," said Harvey. "One of them was a guy? And why are you calling people we don't know witches? I'm sure they were nice."

"Right." I sighed. "I was jealous and stupid. I thought and did jealous, stupid things. I'm sorry, Harvey. I didn't think about you at all. I was caught up in worrying that everything would change after I turn sixteen. I know we aren't official or anything, and I'm getting ahead of myself, but even if everything does change, I want us to keep seeing each other."

He was silent. Maybe he was horrified. Surely he wasn't horrified.

I risked a glance upward. He was clearly horrified.

"We aren't *official* or anything?" he breathed.

"Um," I said. "Look—"

"Are you trying to tell me that you're *not* my girlfriend? But I—I've been telling people you're my girlfriend for a year! I told people at the face-painting stall that you were my girlfriend. I told my great-aunt Mildred you're my girlfriend, and she lives in a nursing home in Florida and she asks after you every time she calls! Sabrina, I totally respect your choices, but if you didn't want to be my girlfriend, I w-wish you'd mentioned it before now."

Harvey's voice caught in his throat.

"Wait," I said.

"Do you want to see other people?" Harvey continued in ever more dismayed tones.

"No!" I exclaimed. "*No.* I want to be your girlfriend. Am I your girlfriend? Are you my boyfriend? Is that what's going on?"

"I..." Harvey faltered. "I thought it was."

"For a year. Why didn't you ask me to be your girlfriend?"

"Why didn't you ask me to be your boyfriend?" Harvey shot back. Then he softened as he always did, worried he would hurt someone with even the smallest of sharp comments. He ducked his head until he caught my eye, and when he did, the dismay melted from his face. "'Brina, I was too terrified to even ask you out! I ended up organizing a friendly trip to the movies, and then calling Roz and Susie and asking them not to come with. I'd tried to do it like ten times before."

Now Harvey mentioned it, I realized he'd suggested going to the movies a lot around then. Like, every few days. Once to see a nature documentary. I'd gone every time. I hadn't even questioned it. I'd just thought that he wanted us all to learn interesting facts about sea lions.

I'd only wanted to be with him.

Maybe what he was saying was true.

And maybe he was saying this because of the spell I'd done. I would never know.

"That's good to hear," I said numbly.

The tiny, encouraging smile was fading from his mouth, because I wasn't smiling back. Harvey's gaze searched my face.

"Wait a second," he said, and threw down his schoolbag, and knelt in the long grass by the well. "You said you remembered this place."

My eyes drifted to the river, the quiet, shining surface that hid a girl's green coat, and another girl's diamond ring, and the bones.

"Um, yes," I said. "Vaguely."

"I was so surprised when we found the well on our class trip," Harvey told me. "I felt like it might be a sign. Like it might be—stop me if this sounds silly—a wishing well."

"It doesn't sound silly to me."

Harvey's fingers threaded through the grass, and loose earth, and stray stones. "I liked you so much, and I didn't know how to tell you. I drew a picture of this place, and you said you liked the picture, so I gave it to you, and you said you'd keep it. I thought maybe at last, I'd find the courage to ask you out. I made a wish."

Harvey stood in the tall grass by the little stone well, and then came back through the long grass to me. He offered his hand to me again, but this time he didn't want me to hold it.

This time he was holding out an offering. There was a small gray stone in the hollow of his palm. Slowly, I reached out and took the stone.

It was worn by a year's worth of time and rain, but I could still make out what was scratched on the smooth gray surface of the stone. My name, *Sabrina*, and beneath the name a swiftly scratched sketch of a rose. It couldn't have been drawn by anyone but my romantic artist.

A year of time and rain. My name. His wish. The stone was like a nugget of gold in my hand.

Harvey gave me the same shy smile he'd given me ten years ago when I approached a strange boy on my first day of school.

"I tried to throw the stone in the wishing well, but I missed," he confessed. "Tommy always told me I don't have a great throwing arm. I chickened out on asking you out that day, and too many days after. I should've asked you to the movies and said it was a date, but I was too chicken for that as well. I never dreamed you would ever doubt how much I liked you. I was only worried you wouldn't want *me*."

I shook my head, my throat closing up, my vision shining with tears. I closed my fingers tight around the stone.

"A year ago you were my only wish," Harvey whispered. "After our first kiss, I knew I didn't ever want to kiss anyone else. After our first day of school, I went home and told my brother I was going to marry you."

I blinked. Harvey bit his lip.

"Oh God, that's weird, isn't it? You think that's weird. I'm so sorry. I was five. Please remember that I was five. Seriously, Sabrina, I know I've been acting bizarrely this past week. I don't know what I was thinking. It was like—I wasn't afraid of anything, and I could take all the risks I wanted to. It's kind of fuzzy now. I guess it was a reaction to being worried about Tommy leaving, but I went way overboard. There's no excuse."

"It wasn't your fault," I said. "It was m—wait, you think you went overboard?"

He hadn't said I was beautiful as the morning today, or yesterday. He'd called me 'Brina, the little pet name he hadn't used when he was rhapsodizing about what a goddess I was. He hadn't been embarrassed when he was singing the song or paying me excessive compliments or making the flower wreaths, but he'd apologized yesterday. He was embarrassed now.

I didn't know how, and I didn't know why, but I was sure of one thing. He wasn't enchanted anymore.

"I know I did." A deep flush ran along the tops of Harvey's cheekbones. "The stuff I said, I mean, of course I think those things whenever I see you, but I know it's over the top to say it, and it sounds ridiculous, and then there were the flowers, and then there was that awful *song*—I'm sure your family told you about the song—"

"They didn't mention anything about a song," I lied firmly. "I don't know anything about a song."

"Oh, good," said Harvey. "Never mind the song. Please never ask me about it. I can't believe I acted that way. And I can't believe that you didn't know how I feel about you, all because I was too scared to come out and say it. I'll be different from now on. I'll try really hard not to be chicken again."

I came to a decision.

"I'll try too," I promised him. "I'm not going to doubt you again, and I'm not going to doubt myself either."

Harvey gave a soft laugh. "You? You never seem afraid of anything."

"You'd be surprised," I said. "But I'll try not to be afraid anymore."

"Then I bet you'll never be afraid again."

I laughed too. "What would you bet?"

"I'd bet all I have on you. I'm not sure of much," said Harvey. "I am sure of you. I always have been."

I put the stone in my pocket and reached out both my hands for him. He clasped my hands in his, smiling down at me with exactly the same wonder he'd shown when he was enchanted, with the same wonder he'd felt all along. Now he was a little more shy, a little more hesitant, and it was so much better, because I knew it was real.

"Hey, Harvey," I asked. "Do you want to be my boyfriend?"

Harvey laughed, and leaned down, and kissed me. "Yeah," he murmured against my lips. "Yes. I really do."

I felt his laughter ripple against my mouth, like a river, like a song. I clung to his jacket and stood on tiptoes to reach him, he leaned down to me, and the arch of our bodies was like the arch of the branches above. Harvey's gaze was too often shadowed, but when he was happy, when he was looking at me as he was now, there were lights in his brownish hazel eyes that made them look golden as the leaves over our heads. I wondered why I'd ever dreaded the leaves turning, when gold was the color of victory, the color of bright, blazing joy.

One day, perhaps Harvey would tell me that he loved me, and I would know he meant it, and that it was real. One day, perhaps I could tell him I was a witch, like he had told me the secrets of his family, and he would believe me, and we would start on a new adventure together.

On our way to school, I walked through the woods beside my mortal boyfriend, wearing my red coat as a flag of defiance. A challenge from the half mortal, issued to every demon or spirit or witch hiding in the darkness, and to the unknown future.

Go on. Come and get me. You're welcome to try.

✳✳✳

Harvey's brother picked us up and dropped me home in his truck.

"We're changing to the winter shift next week," Tommy warned as we scrambled into the truck. "No more getting chauffeured for you, nerd."

"Nice while it lasted," said Harvey. "Eyes on the road, driver."

I smacked Harvey in the arm and he gave me a quick kiss, and behind the wheel Tommy laughed. We drove up the curving road to home with me tucked under Harvey's arm, warm even though the wind had a bite of coming winter in it.

Ambrose was sitting on the porch railing in his red dressing gown and black jeans, looking at his laptop. He flipped the lap-top closed as the truck pulled up, and grinned.

"Tommy. Harvey. Thanks for bringing Sabrina home. Auntie Hilda's made her famous eyeball lasagna, cousin. You don't want to miss that."

I made a warning face.

"Hey, Ambrose." Tommy grinned shyly back and leaned against the wheel. "It's no problem. Your aunt's what lasagna?"

"Aubergine lasagna," Ambrose corrected himself hastily. "I said *aubergine*. Americans call aubergines eggplants, but that's ridiculous. You don't get eggs from plants. It's, um . . . a vegetarian dish." He nodded, smile growing unnervingly wide in his attempt to seem charmingly normal.

Harvey squinted at him. Tommy, a trusting soul, was still grinning as if he thought Ambrose was hilarious and harmless.

"Okay," said Tommy indulgently. "I'm sure it's delicious."

"Delicious is a strong word," I said. "But I like a family dinner. Bye, boyfriend."

Harvey gave me a secret, delighted smile. "Bye, girlfriend."

Ambrose made a gagging sound, but in an amused way. I scrambled out of the truck, and Ambrose leaped lightly down onto the porch steps to join me, laptop tucked under his arm.

Harvey and Tommy both had the same look in their eyes for a moment, Harvey's grave and dark and Tommy's sunny blue: almost wistful. I thought again that I wished I knew

Tommy better, that our families could know each other better. I wished I could ask them both inside to share our family meal.

Aunt Zelda wasn't good at acting like a mortal for long stretches of time. She definitely wouldn't appreciate me inviting two mortals over for dinner without any notice.

Harvey climbed out of the truck and got in front with Tommy, and Tommy slung an arm around Harvey's shoulders. They were okay, I told myself. They had each other. They were going home together.

I waved goodbye to both brothers and watched the cherry-red truck disappear around the curve of the road, under the golden leaves. Someday in the future, when I'd told Harvey the truth, perhaps I could invite them for dinner.

One day. Maybe.

Ambrose, whose default when dealing with mortals was to flirt with them or dismiss them or flirtatiously dismiss them, turned away without another glance. I hurried up the porch steps after him and into the house.

"Hey, could I have a word alone with you?"

Ambrose wiggled his eyebrows. "Sounds ominous. All right."

He gestured to the split-level staircase that rose from our hall, the right and left sides of the stairs mirroring each other. We sat down side by side on the red-carpeted steps.

"The spell on Harvey," I said. "It's gone. I think it was gone yesterday."

Ambrose made a humming sound. "Thought it might be. Honestly, I'm surprised it lasted this long. The spell breaks with true love's kiss, you see. Very classic. Very traditional."

The spell hadn't broken when Harvey and I kissed on the Ferris wheel at the Last Day of Summer fair. Maybe I'd still been thinking too much about myself back then.

I remembered the day of thorns and roses, how I'd kissed Harvey's hands, and then recalled Tommy kissing his brother's hair. Maybe it had been me, and maybe it had been Tommy, saving his brother without even knowing, the way Ms. Wardwell saved people by the river. There were so many kinds of love.

"I see. And what was the last line of the spell?"

"Quos amor verus tenuit, tenebit," recited Ambrose. *"True love will hold on to those whom it has held.* If he already loved you all along, then you'd know. If he didn't . . . then you'd know that too. I was fairly confident he did, having seen him give you constant cow's eyes for ten years. I thought it would be a happy surprise for you. I didn't expect river demons. Nobody ever expects river demons."

Tenebit, not *tenebris*. All along, the words had meant *holding*, not *shadows*. It had been my cousin trying to do something nice for me. Not in a normal, mortal way, but we were witches. Ambrose was who he was. I wouldn't have wanted him to be any different.

Still, I wasn't a child he could play with or indulge, not

anymore. And I had to understand him, rather than idolize him or fear him. Now I was growing up, we had to understand each other, even if that was difficult because we were so different. We had to learn to be equals.

But still family. Always family.

"I was proud of you for tricking the demon with your little no-drowning spell," Ambrose told me. "Where did you learn to be tricksy?"

"From the best," I said, and watched the slow smile blossom on Ambrose's face.

When I was a kid, I hadn't worried about Ambrose not reaching out or holding on to me. I just went to him, grabbed hold of him, assumed I was welcome. I'd felt the same absolute confidence yesterday when I ran for home and safety. Yesterday when I was in trouble, all doubts had fallen away. Yesterday when I was in trouble, Ambrose had held on tight to me.

Today I slid my arm around Ambrose's waist, and rested my cheek against his silk-clad shoulder.

"I'm sorry I was horrible before."

"I was horrible too," said Ambrose easily. "Witches sometimes are. Anyway, you were punished. Now you know the awful truth that the secret wish of Harvey's heart is to serenade you with appalling love songs. I'm so sorry you had to find that out. I understand if you can never see him in the same way again."

Of course I think those things whenever I see you.

Harvey had more or less said the influence of the spell on him had made him feel like he wasn't afraid to tell me those things, or to take risks. It was strange and sweet to realize that when Harvey murmured a shy hey to me, or was quiet, or was chatting about comics and movies, he was secretly thinking that I was beautiful as the morning and he wanted to sing me songs and bedeck the world with flowers in my honor.

I didn't need him to do any of that. It was enough to know he wanted to.

"I like that he sang me a song."

Ambrose made a doubtful sound. "Maybe you'd feel differently if you actually heard what the song said. Want me to sing it to you? I can sing it to you right now."

I headbutted him gently in the shoulder. "No, I'll wait for Harvey to tell me how he feels himself. I'm glad he loves me. I really love him. I'll tell him that someday too."

"I've heard love can overcome anything," Ambrose remarked. "I suppose that includes tone deafness."

I hit his arm. He cackled, my cousin, the wicked witch of any direction he could find. Maybe we wouldn't be family in the same way if he wasn't trapped here, but here he was. Even though he was trapped here, he could've ignored me or avoided me. Instead he'd opened his grimoire for me and taught me my first spells. When I was four, I would lift my hands up to him and he would laugh and pick me up and carry me around the house. When I was fourteen, he would laugh and talk to me about boys.

I'd grown up with dreams of home and my parents, but they were dreams. In all my true memories of home, he was there. I'd found myself doubting a lot recently, but there were some things I never doubted.

I took a deep breath. "Do you know what else I love?"

"Hairbands?" suggested Ambrose.

I burst out laughing, and understood anew why Ambrose laughed so much. Laughter threw a challenge at pain, and sometimes defeated it.

Ambrose laughed with me. "It is hairbands, isn't it?"

"It's you. I really love you."

Ambrose stopped laughing. Silence followed my words, broken only by the faraway clatter of pans from the kitchen, and the murmur of my aunts' voices, the creaks of old floorboards and doors complaining to themselves, and faintest of all, the noise of leaves rustling around our slanted rooftops. The sounds of home.

Soft as the light stealing through our stained glass windows, he said: "I love you back, Sabrina. With all my cold, fickle witch's heart."

My throat closed up so I couldn't speak for a moment. I rubbed my cheek against his shoulder.

He hesitated. Even more quietly, he added: "When I let you down, I won't mean to."